CHRISTMAS IN THE SISTERS

A *Holiday Mystery Novel*

Book Six in The Sisters, Texas Mystery Series

Becki Willis

ISBN: 1947686003
ISBN 13: 9781947686007

BOOKS BY BECKI WILLIS

The Sisters, Texas Mystery Series
Chicken Scratch
When the Stars Fall
Stipulations and Complications
Home Again: Starting Over
Genny's Ballad
Christmas in The Sisters: A Holiday Mystery Novel
Mirrors Don't Lie Series
The Girl from Her Mirror
Mirror, Mirror on Her Wall
Light from Her Mirror
Forgotten Boxes
Tangible Spirits
He Kills Me, He Kills Me Not

1

Emergency lights clashed with the festive Christmas scene.

Beyond the police car's glaring strobe, cheerful strands of twinkling white icicles dripped from the eaves of the house. Each porch post was wrapped in green. A profusion of multi-color lights sprang up in the yard, garnishing every bush, every bird feeder, and every tree in sight.

Wedging the cruiser into a slim niche between a Ford Expedition and a Pontiac Grand Am, Brash deCordova came within inches of a gigantic inflatable snowman. The chief of police picked his way between a stand of lighted candy canes, a herd of reindeer, and an animated gingerbread man. The obstacle course led him to the front porch, where a trio of wooden carolers greeted him, and a motion-activated wreath began the first bars of *We Wish You a Merry Christmas*.

It came as no surprise when the doorbell twinkled out the tune of *Jingle Bells*. Brash shook his head in wonder. The Hutchins certainly loved the season.

The door swung open and a plump woman motioned him inside. "Brash! You're here." The relief in Vanessa Hutchins' voice was palatable. "Come in, come in." She turned slightly away and bellowed down the hall, "Larry! The police are here!"

"I'm sorry to come calling like this, Vanessa," Brash apologized, tugging the cowboy hat from his auburn head. "Larry tells me you've had some trouble."

"I'll say! Look! Just look at that!" She flung her arm toward the massive Christmas tree centered at the front windows. Dozens of bulbs, baubles, and ornaments covered every tip, illuminated by hundreds of miniature white lights. A red and green tree skirt peeked from beneath the lower branches.

"Nice tree," Brash murmured, wondering how it kept from collapsing.

"Nice? It's empty! Glory be, someone stole all our presents!"

A groove of worry puckered the officer's brow. "All of them? How many did you have under there?"

"You mean an exact number?"

"For now, an estimate will do."

Vanessa cocked her head to one side, mentally tallying up the gifts. "At least thirty. I'm almost done with my shopping. Or I was, until *this* happened!" She gave another emphatic wave toward the barren tree skirt.

"Calm down, Nessa," her husband said, coming into the room carrying a steaming mug. He thrust it at his wife before offering his hand to Brash. "Brash, thanks for coming out so quick. Vanessa, take a few sips of hot chocolate and try to relax. Everything is going to be all right."

"All right? You're not the one who shopped for those gifts. And you didn't wrap a single one of them, Larry, so don't tell me to calm down!" Her voice rose with every word, both in pitch and volume.

"Can we have a seat?" Brash suggested.

Appalled by her lack of manners, the frantic woman immediately turned apologetic. She fussed around the officer, fluffing a snowman afghan at his back and producing a Santa-shaped ottoman for his feet. Brash politely settled among the excessive holiday pillows, grimacing when he activated one with music. Over the digital notes of *Rudolph the Red Nosed Reindeer*, he struggled to sound professional. "Tell me exactly what happened."

"We were robbed, that's what happened!"

"Were there any signs of forced entry?"

"The back door was jimmied open, if that's what you mean," Larry Hutchins offered. "We didn't touch anything, in case you want to dust for prints."

"Smart thinking. Was anything else taken?"

"Not that we're aware of. We checked the gun case, jewelry box, desk drawers where we keep the checkbook, that sort of thing. Everything else seems to be here."

"They were only interested in the presents," his wife concurred. Hot chocolate already forgotten, she had taken to wringing her hands.

Brash jotted down notes in his trusty little notebook. It traveled with him everywhere he went, tucked into his shirt pocket. "Take me through this evening. We need to establish some sort of timeline."

"Well, let's see... I got off work around four. I stopped by Granny Bert Cessna's to leave a donation for the Angel Tree. Bless her heart, that woman is over eighty and still as active as ever! She told me she's going to Vegas to attend the National

Finals Rodeo with her new beau, Sticker Pierce. They're doing some big award for him, being as he's a rodeo legend and all. Glory be! Anyway, on the way home, I spotted Glitter Thompson walking her dogs, so I stopped to chat for a few minutes. Poor dear is having trouble with her bursitis again. So, I must have wound up getting home about five fifteen or so. Since I forgot to lay anything out for dinner, we decided to go out for supper when Larry came home."

Brash waded through all the useless chatter to find a kernel or two of helpful information. "Were the gifts still under the tree when you arrived home at five fifteen?"

"Yes. The first thing I do when I get home is turn on the tree lights. I've thought of getting one of those automatic timers, but I'm not sure I trust them."

"What time did Larry get in?"

"Five thirty-eight, same as every day. You can set your clock by this man." For the first time since Brash had arrived, Vanessa smiled. She patted her husband's shoulder as she stood over him, too nervous to sit.

"And neither of you saw anything unusual? No strangers about, no cars out front, no unscheduled deliveries?" Brash clarified.

"No, everything seemed normal," Larry answered.

"What time did you leave for the restaurant?"

"Around six thirty. And we called you the minute we got in, about ten minutes ago."

"So that narrows down the window of opportunity to about an hour and thirty-five minutes."

Larry nodded. "That sounds about right."

"Vanessa, do you have a list of everything under the tree?"

"Of course. I keep a detailed list of what I buy for each person, and I check each item off as I wrap it. I'll be happy to get it for you."

"Fine, fine. But I'd like to ask a few more questions before you do. Have either of you noticed anything strange over the past several days, or weeks? Again, any strangers about, cars out front, deliveries, anything disturbed in the yard, anything at all?"

"I don't believe so."

"Glory be, not that I can think of."

"How long has your tree been up?"

"We always put it up Thanksgiving evening, while the kids are here to help pull things out of the attic. Larry's shoulder gives him a fit, you know. Rheumatism."

"Old football injury," her husband claimed, rotating his arm as if to disprove his wife's claims.

Brash had been a few years behind the other man in school, but he knew Larry Hutchins did little more than warm the bench. The most strenuous thing he ever did during a football game was to carry the water cooler and hoist it in victory when the Cotton Kings won, dumping its contents on the coach's head.

Himself Cotton King royalty, Brash chose to ignore the exaggeration. Instead, he turned to Vanessa. "How long have the gifts been under there?"

"I couldn't start wrapping without paper, of course, and I didn't decide on my theme until after Black Friday."

"Theme?"

She bobbed her head. "I do a different theme of paper each year, you know, and this time it was snowflakes. You should have seen the tree... it was particularly gorgeous this year, with at least six different snowflake papers in all different colors." Her eyes turned misty as she clasped her hands over her heart and mourned the lost beauty. The monetary loss hadn't been mentioned yet, most likely because she was still in the emotional phase of the theft. "As soon as I settled on a theme, I went to Bryan and bought all my paper."

"And when was that?"

"Let's see... It wasn't Monday, and I don't think it was Tuesday, because I had a Weight Off meeting. I had church on Wednesday night and played Bunco on Thursday." She scrunched her face as she ran through her week. She had a brief argument with herself about whether she had missed the Wednesday night service, until she remembered Brother Greer's lesson. She even went so far as to share the gist of it with the two men. When she still couldn't pin down the exact day she went shopping, she called in reinforcement. "Larry, what day did I bring home dinner from *Tasty's?*"

"What's *Tasty's?*" Her husband looked perplexed.

"That new fast food place on the way out of Bryan, the one with those low-cal smoothies I'm always raving about." When he still looked confused, she added, "You know, where Merle Bishop's granddaughter started working." Nothing registered on his face. With an exasperated sigh, she found something he could relate to. "The spicy chicken wings, Larry. What night did I bring them home?"

"Oh, Tuesday night," her husband readily supplied. "I had already eaten at the poker game, but they made a nice midnight snack."

The mention of a poker game did not escape Brash's attention, but he made no comment. For the better part of the past year, he had been chasing a gambling ring operating in and around The Sisters. The operation included poker games, cock fighting, and some serious football score pools. To his consternation, he had yet to make a solid arrest, but he was getting close. He could feel it.

With a mental note to ask about the game later, Brash focused on the crime at hand. "So, you purchased the paper on Tuesday and began wrapping shortly after that. Now, I want both of you to think about this carefully. Since last Tuesday, has there been anyone in the house that normally doesn't visit? A repairman, perhaps, or a neighbor who surprised you by dropping by? A delivery man who offered to bring the packages inside?"

"I had someone come in and work on my cuckoo clock. Every year, I have the little bird replaced with a Santa for the holidays." Vanessa glanced at her watch. "He should be making an appearance in about five minutes."

"We had a new freezer delivered and set up yesterday," Larry said. "I'm taking a taxidermy class and need a place to keep mounts before I work on them."

"And of course, I hosted Bunco on Thursday. There's sixteen in our group," Vanessa supplied. She nodded her head vigorously. "Yes, I remember now. Glory be, I was so shook up, I couldn't even think earlier. But yes, I bought the paper Tuesday night and I took off work on Thursday so I could binge-wrap presents. I wanted the tree to look perfect when the ladies came."

Brash held in a groan. He had his work cut out for him, running down all these potential leads. "Anyone else you can think of that has been in or around the house in the past week?"

"I hired a couple of high school boys to help me hang lights."

"The Avon lady dropped off my order. And I invited the paper boy in while I found my wallet and paid him."

"So, half the town of Juliet has been here," Brash muttered beneath his breath. To the Hutchins, he announced, "I'll need the names of everyone you've mentioned, plus phone numbers if you have them. I'll look at the back door, take a few photos, and write up my report. I'm sure the insurance adjuster will ask for it."

"Insurance?" Vanessa blinked in surprise.

"Your homeowner's policy most likely includes theft. You'll need to call your agent to confirm."

"Glory be, I hadn't even thought of that!"

While Vanessa still looked dazed, her husband's expression lightened considerably. "So, we might not be out all that money, after all?"

Brash stood from the couch, again setting off the musical pillow. "You'll have to speak to your agent to be certain. If you'll direct me to the kitchen, I'll finish up and get out of your way for the evening."

Thirty minutes later, Brash pulled out from their driveway, his ears still ringing. There had been more Hutchins cheer to behold.

On his way through the hall, Brash activated an entire collection of dancing, singing elves. Twice. A tiny little Santa not only popped out from the cuckoo clock, but he chirped *HoHo, HoHo.* In the kitchen, a radio belted out holiday music. The mat at the back door sang the opening notes of *Over the River and Through the Woods*. And as word of the break-in spread, Vanessa's phone kept up a steady jingle with her holiday ringtone. By the time Brash made his way through the maze of dazzling lights and blow-up lawn decor, he welcomed the peace and quiet of his patrol car. He never thought the squawk of a police scanner could be considered peaceful, but then again, he had never visited the Hutchins' home at Christmastime.

Glory be.

2

"How does this look?" Madison Reynolds stood back and surveyed the garland in question. "Go up a tiny bit on your left."

Her best friend and current houseguest, Genesis Baker, moved the strand of greenery, almost as directed.

"Your other left," Madison motioned with a grin. "There. Perfect."

"See? Who needs Kiki Paretta when you have the off-kilter stylings of Genny and Maddy?" Genny's dimples deepened as she stood back to inspect their handiwork.

"I was tempted to take her up on her offer, you know," Maddy confessed. "Christmas decorations for a house this size is appallingly expensive, but I couldn't bear the thought of doing another television show."

"It would have only been one episode, not a full season like before."

"It hasn't even been two months, Gen, since we did the final reveal. I'm thinking it might be two decades before I'm ready to go through *that* again!"

That was having her very own reality show on HOME TV, centered around the restoration of her hundred-year-old home. Remodeling the historic mansion, known affectionately around town as the Big House, was a huge hit on national television, but it left much to be desired in the way of privacy. Even though the cameras were gone, life still hadn't returned to normal in the tiny sister towns of Naomi and Juliet. No way would she agree to appear on *Kreations by Kiki,* even if the designer agreed to donate all decorations.

"At least you took *By the Yard* up on their offer. Your lights are going to be amazing!" Genny predicted.

"They've done a great job with the lawn," Madison agreed. "If they want to branch off into custom holiday lighting and use my house for advertising, I'm more than willing. I would never attempt to string lights on a three-story house by myself."

"I can't wait to see the finished project! They said they'd be done by tomorrow evening." Excitement sparkled within Genny's baby-blue eyes and she clapped her hands together. "Oh, I know! We can have a lighting party! We'll invite everyone over for snacks, and then we'll go outside and let you flip the switch, for oohs and aahs all around."

"With my luck, it will turn out to be like the scene from *Christmas Vacation,* when Chevy Chase plugs in the cord and nothing happens!" Maddy laughed as she recalled the oldie-but-goldie movie, as her son Blake called it. She aimed an accusing look at her friend. "Besides, you just want an excuse to throw a party. Now that you're back to your old self again, you seem to be stuck in hostess mode."

Genny tried to wipe the smile from her face, but it refused to budge. "Sorry," she claimed, but it was an empty apology. "I'm just so over the moon. I've honestly never been this happy in my entire life. I guess I just want to share it with the world!"

Maddy gave her friend an impulsive hug. "If anyone deserves happiness, it's you, my dear friend. You've had a rough time lately, so it's nice to see this smile back on your face." She wondered if she could be as resilient as Genny, if their positions were reversed.

True, Maddy had been through her own trials this past year. Widowed at the age of thirty-nine. Left penniless, thanks to her late husband. Driven from her home and her life in Dallas. Forced to move back home to live with her grandmother. Starting over had been the hardest thing she had ever done, but she had managed. Granny Bert sold her the Big House for a token five thousand dollars, agreed to finance it, and promptly coerced the master carpenter at HOME TV to take on the renovation, all at no cost to Maddy. There was a price to pay, of course—no privacy, public exploitation, public ridicule—but the result was worth it. She and her twins had a home. They had a future.

Part of starting over included opening *In a Pinch*, a temporary service to fill in where needed and to perform odd jobs around town. A smile touched Madison's face as she recalled how odd some of those jobs had been! Some had even led to danger. Yet even when her life was threatened, it hadn't been personal, not really. The perpetrators only meant to stop her from uncovering their own nefarious deeds.

But Genny. Poor, sweet Genny. She had been stalked. Kidnapped. Had her home burned to the ground. Attacked with a knife. The deeds had all been deeply personal, committed by a man who claimed to love her, and a woman who vowed to hate her. Wounds like that left deep scars. Madison didn't know if she could have recovered the way Genny had.

After a brief stint of depression, her friend bounced back from the darkness and was once again her sunny, optimistic self. Genesis Baker was a strong woman, and the best friend Madison could ever hope to have.

"No matter how hard I try, I can't seem to swallow this smile," Genny confessed. "Someone came into the cafe yesterday and told me this really sad story, and it was all I could do not to break out in song. I'm so crazy happy, it's not even funny."

"Your hunk of a fiancé has the same problem. I saw Cutter yesterday, working a wreck, and he had that same goofy smile on his face the entire time."

"Hey, I resent that!" Genny pretended to sulk. "My smile is not goofy. It's—It's… love inspired. Just like yours is, whenever Brash is around."

Instead of smiling, Maddy frowned. "Yes, well, you may not have noticed, but that hasn't been all that much these last couple of weeks."

Genny busied herself, carefully arranging a casual collection of antique ornaments inside a tall glass vase. "And why is that?" she asked.

"He's been so busy lately, chasing down this gambling ring. It's almost like he's obsessed."

"A man like Brash deCordova is used to success. Look at his past. Star football player in high school. Big shot in college ball. A career in the pros. Successful college coach for two major universities. Now he's chief of police and special investigator for the county. A leader like that doesn't take defeat well, and you know he has to see this organized gambling ring as defeat." She stepped back to critique her work.

Maddy reluctantly agreed. "I suppose. And maybe it's just as well he's so busy right now. Things have been a little strained with Bethani lately."

"I picked up on that." Genny topped the collection off with a snowman ornament, handblown from mercury glass.

"Ooh, I like that," Maddy approved. "That looks really good."

"I'll put the rest in that cut crystal bowl, put it on the other table, and call it good. Classic and understated, but festive."

"Sounds like a plan."

As Genny started the next project, she asked, "So what gives with Bethani?"

Madison placed graceful bows at even intervals among the fireplace garland. The front parlor was the most formal of the rooms in the Big House, and therefore the room she spent the least amount of time in. Still, it needed a touch of holiday spirit, particularly since it spilled into the formal dining room. That, too, was reserved for special occasions, and what occasion was more special than Christmas? She agreed with Genny on how to decorate these two rooms. Less, in this case, was more.

Concentrating on her spacing, Madison spoke over her shoulder. "I can answer that in one word. Annette. Spending time with my mother-in-law is like being exposed to small doses of poison. Over time, it builds in your system and becomes toxic."

"I can understand Annette spouting her usual nonsense, but Bethani likes Brash. I thought she was okay with your relationship."

"I thought so, too," Maddy sighed as she tied the final bow. "But she's sixteen. It's an impressionable age. And she adored her father. Going back to Dallas, seeing his headstone, hearing all the sentimental stories Annette told…"

"It's only natural, Maddy," Genny reassured her friend. "Holidays are an emotional time of year. Of course, she misses her dad."

"Last year was so hard, you know? Gray had just been killed, and our world was crashing down around us. We went through the motions of the holidays, but our hearts weren't in it. Between trying to hold it together and trying to protect the kids from all the sordid details, it felt like Christmas came and went without me even knowing it. I was really looking forward to the holidays this year and now… now this. I feel like I take one step forward, two steps back."

Genny advanced toward her friend, grabbed her arm, and dragged her along as she stepped off two long, forward paces. "There. Two steps forward, not a single one back. This is going to be an amazing Christmas, just you wait and see."

Maddy smiled at Genny's enthusiasm. If anyone could will it to be so, it was her friend.

"We've gotten a good start on it," she admitted. "The room looks great. And I am pleased to say, we are now officially done with our decorating." She dusted her hands for good measure.

"All the more reason for a lighting party tomorrow night, don't you think?" Genny asked with an impish grin.

Maddy shook her head in defeat, but she was smiling. "Okay, okay. We can have a lighting party."

Genny's dimples appeared again. "You'll see, Maddy. This is one Christmas you'll never forget!"

As darkness settled in over the town, a festive group gathered on the front lawns of the Big House.

"This is going to be so awesome!" Megan deCordova predicted, giggling as only a teenager could do. She and Bethani linked arms as they awaited the big moment.

"You should have seen how they put the lights up on the top gables." At sixteen, her twin brother Blake was more intrigued by the hydraulic lifts than he was by the twinkling lights. He and best friend Jamil Green launched into a vivid recount of the scene, engaging anyone who would listen. As chief of the volunteer fire department, Cutter Montgomery knew the most about the equipment used. He and the teens swapped stories about hydraulic options and motors, with occasional input from Megan's stepfather Matthew Aikman.

"Nearly done!" Derron Mullins called to the group.

Before leaving, the tech from *By the Yard* had assured Madison that everything was set. One touch of the remote, and she would have lights. But there had been an incident after the installers left; the Hadleys' goat had gotten loose and wandered onto the corner estate. After a light snack of electrical cords and connectors, the goat proceeded to tangle the remaining cords unmercifully. By the time Madison discovered the mess, the lawn and lighting experts were on the other side of the county. She frantically called her part-time employee and friend, Derron, to help her sort it all out. With Brash's help, they were almost finished.

"Okay, dollface, we have it," Derron said a few minutes later. "Light 'er up."

Wanting the twins to be a part of the moment, she motioned them closer. "Blake, Beth, let's do this together."

"Okay, everybody, start the countdown!" someone suggested.

The crowd called out as a single voice. "Ten. Nine. Eight."

Madison gave the twins a quick hug as the numbers fell. She held the master remote, and their hands supported hers.

"Four. Three. Two."

"This is a new beginning for us, guys," Maddy whispered. "Our future is as bright as these lights." With hope shining in her hazel eyes, she pressed the button.

The lights were dazzling, but not overpowering. Some twinkled, some burned steady. Thousands of soft white bulbs traced the graceful bones of the old mansion. Electronic icicles fell from the eaves and gables of every porch, every soffit, appearing to drip in the night. More lights traced the silhouette of each turret. Taking cues from the paint pallet, most of the lights were white, but accents of red echoed the house's cranberry trim. The contrasting colors wrapped around the many porch posts and spindles. The lights lit the dark sky around it, making the house appear to glow like a beacon in the night.

Madison's heart swelled. This was her beacon.

Another beacon in her life, Brash moved through the crowd so that he stood behind her. "Gorgeous, isn't it?" he murmured over her shoulder.

"Oh, Brash, have you ever seen anything so beautiful?" Madison breathed the words as she leaned back into his warmth. "I still have moments when this all seems surreal. Sometimes I can't believe that something so beautiful belongs to me."

"I know what you mean," he murmured softly, but his eyes were on her, not the house.

Maddy didn't notice his double meaning. She was still enchanted with the house. "They did an absolutely amazing job. I don't think I've ever seen anything like it, have you?"

"It's perfect," he agreed. "This is how Christmas lights should be done, not like the ones over at the Hutchins'. Theirs are like Santa's elves on steroids." He cringed with the memory. "But these lights are perfect. Not too gaudy, not too flashy. Understated elegance, just like the house. And its new owner."

She smiled at his compliment. "Thank you, but you might be a bit prejudiced."

"Maybe," he agreed. Slipping his arms around her, he leaned even closer and whispered confidentially, "I'm in love with the owner, you know."

A mischievous smile played upon her lips. "Yes, I believe I heard something about that. Of course, my memory is rather sketchy. I might need reminding later."

His voice dropped to a sexy purr, sending shivers of delight across her skin. "I would love to give you an in-depth demonstration."

Maddy's heart quickened with the low timbre of his words. She hugged his arms to her. "We never seem to have any alone time," she complained.

"I know, sweetheart. Things have been hectic." He gave her a squeeze. "Our time is coming, sweetheart. I promise."

"I will hold you to that, Mr. deCordova."

"I'm looking forward to Christmas with you, Maddy." She loved the feel of his deep voice rumbling against her. She loved the way her name fell from his lips, the way his low voice made anything sound sensual.

"It's going to be awesome," she whispered.

They stood in silence, soaking in the inner warmth that somehow emanated from the lights. After a few moments, Brash's deep baritone filled the air as he began the first strands of *Silent Night*. One by one, other voices joined in, but

Maddy was one of the last to pitch in. She found her throat clogged with emotion.

This, she thought, *is what Christmas is all about. Love, and home, and family.*

Before the evening was done, the crowd sang every song they knew the words to, and some they didn't. Neighbors came out from along the street to admire the house and the impromptu caroling. Maddy invited everyone back inside to finish the refreshments and to partake in some of Genny's special eggnog.

And just like that, a new tradition in The Sisters was born.

3

Madison was surprised when Brash sent her a text, asking to meet at his office the next morning. She pulled into the old train depot turned police station, worrying that something had happened.

One look at her face, and Brash was quick to say, "I didn't mean to alarm you, sweetheart. There's nothing wrong. At least, not like you're thinking."

She put her hand to her heart. "You know me, the first thing I think is that something happened to the kids."

Brash cleared off the edge of his desk and propped a lean hip against it, stretching long legs out before him. "This has nothing to do with the kids. Actually, it's a police matter."

Madison had been admiring his long, athletic frame, but his words snapped her gaze to his. "Do I have an unpaid parking ticket I know nothing about?"

"Of course not. From a traffic citation perspective, you are a model citizen, my love."

"Somehow that doesn't sound like a compliment. Are you insinuating I'm not always a model citizen?"

"Well," Brash drawled, "there have been a few issues with trespassing. Poking your nose into police business. Getting yourself into some rather peculiar jams."

"Hey, none of those have been of my own choosing. They have been a direct result of my clients' situations."

"Simmer down now. Don't get your feathers ruffled. I didn't bring you here to pick a fight."

"Then why did you bring me down here?" she asked shortly.

"I want to hire you."

It wasn't the first time the police department had retained the services of *In a Pinch*, but his words still surprised her. "Oh. Why didn't you say so?"

A sexy grin slid over his face, threatening to steal her breath away. "Because I like to see that fire in your eyes. You're even more beautiful when you're all riled up."

It was difficult to stay aggravated at him when he said something like that, but she gave it her best shot. "That must be why you keep me riled up so often," she sniffed.

His eyes traveled over her with delicious suggestion. "I certainly try."

She checked the buttons on her blouse, certain he had undone the top few with just his gaze. "Unless you plan to close those blinds, maybe you should tell me what you're talking about."

With a sigh, Brash stood from the desk. His knee popped in protest, a reminder of his days playing football. Madison frowned when she saw his slight limp.

"Are you all right, Brash?" she asked in concern.

"As all right as I can be, seeing as I only have two officers and a growing crime wave on my hands." He plopped down into his chair and sat back with a short exhale. "There was another break-in last night."

"Oh no!"

"I'm sure you know by now, the first was at Larry and Vanessa Hutchins'. Someone broke into the house and stole all the wrapped presents from under the tree. Last night, someone broke into Mona and Reggie Carr's vehicle while it was sitting in their driveway. Mona Carr shopped all day yesterday and hadn't unloaded the car yet. When Reggie went out to unload this morning, someone had beaten him to it."

Madison gasped. "You're kidding! That is terrible!"

Frustration etched into Brash's face. "This sort of thing just doesn't happen around here, Maddy. We're a close-knit, law-abiding community. We look out for our neighbors, not steal from them!"

"Like last night," she nodded. "That was so awesome, the way neighbors up and down the street came out and joined us."

"Exactly. I won't tolerate this kind of unlawfulness in our community." His voice turned to granite. "We have to shut it down, and we have to shut it down now."

"I agree. How can I help?"

"In the past week, the Hutchins have had half the community traipsing through their house, which makes the potential persons of interest list a mile long. The guys and I are busy trying to pin down this illegal gambling ring. I would like to hire *In a Pinch* to check out the people on this list and compare notes on the two thefts. They may or may not be connected. Interested?"

"Of course! I'd like to say I'd do it for free, just to help out, but... I have bills."

"Of course you do. I would never ask you to do this for free."

"People assume that since I did the TV show, I must be rich to go along with the famous. Yes, I got a gorgeous house out of the deal, but it didn't put a penny into my bank account. I have bills, just like everyone else."

"Maddy, you don't have to explain yourself to me. And you know I would help you in any way I can, if you'd just let me." He saw the argument on her face and held up a warning hand. "Let's not get into that discussion again. This is a business proposition, plain and simple. I need help, and you're just the person to do it. Quality work at reasonable rates. Exactly what the taxpayers want."

"Thank you for the vote of confidence. I won't let you down."

He gave her one of his irresistible smiles. "I know. That's why I'm hiring you." He handed her a file. "Here's the information you need. If you need to speak directly to the Hutchins or Carrs, I can set that up for you. Any questions so far?"

"Only a hundred or so. First of which, do you think this is the work of a single perpetrator, or a gang?"

"I'd have to say we're looking at two or more individuals. One to act as lookout, one to go in and make the sweep. The first crime was pulled off in a very specific time frame."

Madison was already jotting down notes. "Do you plan to issue a warning for the public?"

"Not at this time. For all we know, these were two isolated incidents. Someone may have seen opportunity and taken it. There's no reason to alarm folks at this point."

"But people need to know to be vigilant. Keep their door locked, their cars secure, alarms set."

"I would hope they're doing that anyway. But you're right; I could ask the newspaper to run some generic reminder for holiday safety. I just don't want them getting wind of this and making it out to be bigger than it is."

"So, you do or do not think these are related?"

"Officially, at this point, I have no reason to think they are related. But my gut says differently."

"Trust your gut, Brash. Isn't that what you always tell me?"

"I'm glad you've listened."

"I always *listen* to you, Brash. I just don't always take your advice," she added cheekily.

Even though he often accused her of butting into official police business while helping her clients, he had recommended her services to a private investigator. The Houston agency frequently used her as a local contact, and Maddy had tossed around the idea of getting her own PI license. With Brash's help, she was honing her skills as a good investigator and observant detective.

Her sharp mind, however, was the biggest asset in her success. Like now, she was quick to bring up several valid points. Brash discussed each one with her, until the intercom interrupted.

"Yes, Vina?"

"Dane Cessna on line two, Chief. He wants to ask you about the recent Christmas crimes."

Brash groaned aloud, his shoulders sagging in exaggerated disgust. "Too late to keep it out of the presses. Your cousin has already heard."

Maddy made a sad face. "Thanks in part, I'm sure, to our grandmother. You know Granny Bert is all over this." Though no longer mayor of Juliet, Bertha Cessna was still in the loop. Not much happened in either town that slipped the old gal's attention.

"I need to take this, sweetheart. That 'Christmas Crimes' sounds suspiciously like a headline. Not to mention a hashtag."

"I understand. Call me later. Love you." Madison brushed a chaste kiss across his lips and gathered her files.

"Love you, too. Be careful out there, and keep your eyes open." Brash pushed the illuminated button on the phone. As Madison hurried out the door, she heard him greet her cousin, owner and reporter for the local paper. "Dane, hello. Chief deCordova here. What can I do for you?"

Madison stopped at the desk to speak to Vina Jones. There was no determining the black woman's age, but she had been an institution at the police department for as long as anyone could remember. Brash swore that without Vina, the office would fall apart.

At one time intimidated by the woman's scrutinizing gaze, Madison now considered Vina a great ally and an invaluable source of help, if not information. The coordinator might guide Maddy in the right direction, but she never divulged classified details. Vina Jones was a consummate professional.

"Vina, do me a favor."

"Anything, Madison." She qualified her ready response with a cool, "Within my power, of course."

"Of course, Vina. I would never expect anything else." The smile died on her face as Madison shot a worried glance at Brash's closed door and confided, "I'm worried about him, Vina. He's working himself to a frazzle."

"I can't say I don't agree."

"He won't talk to me about it, probably to keep me from worrying so much. But that, of course, only makes me worry more."

Vina nodded in agreement, her face grim. "He's determined to find this gambling ring. It's like he's driven. I've never seen him this way."

"He's asked me to help investigate the recent break-ins, so that he can spend more time on the gambling case. That alone tells me how serious this is."

"I'm glad the chief called you in to help," Vina said with approval. "Now he can focus on shutting down this ring, once and for all. It's been operating for over a year, and every time he thinks he's close, they slip away."

"No wonder he's taking it so personally," she murmured.

"Between us, we'll keep an eye on him," the older woman assured her. "We won't let this get him down. The main thing he needs is plenty of rest, to keep him sharp and focused."

"We can try to make him relax, but Brash deCordova is a stubborn man. It's hard to make him do something he doesn't want to do."

Vina flashed her pearly whites. "The trick, then, is to change what it is he thinks he wants to do, eh?"

Madison was still laughing when she left the building.

Brash dropped the phone back into its cradle. Last night had been a nice reprieve from the pressures of the job, but the morning had wasted no time in reminding him where his duties lay. At least Dane Cessna agreed not to run a sensational story in the paper. He promised to downplay the probability of more thefts, while urging residents to be vigilant during the holidays.

While the thefts were concerning, the lawman's real worry was the increased threat of the gambling ring.

Like in most towns, poker games were common. Even though playing for money was technically illegal, Brash was willing to overlook a friendly wager between friends. Last year, however, there were rumors the games were no longer quite so friendly and the wagers no longer so small. There was mention of known hard-core gamblers involved. Hints of organized crime. Some said that Ronny Gleason invited the unsavory element into the game, but with his death last January, the rumors had faded. So had the games. A few continued to pop up here and there, mostly in other parts of the county, but Brash heard no more reports of cockfighting. Things had cooled down, at least until recently.

Now the poker games were back. Brash didn't think it was a coincidence that Tom Haskell was released from prison over the summer. Even from behind bars, the man had managed to keep his fingers in organized gambling. Tom may or may not have been the one behind the initial move into the county, but Brash had no doubt the man would soon make an appearance. Where the money went, the criminals were sure to follow.

Gambling wasn't the only thing that worried Brash. As always, there was the very real threat of drugs. More than a threat, it was a reality. No town, no matter how small or how safe, was immune to the ugly beast.

It rankled Brash that during last spring's big drug bust, the top boss had gotten away. Maddy and Derron had inadvertently stumbled upon a meth lab, which led to the arrest of several cooks and dealers. While any arrest meant one less lowlife on the street, letting the boss slip through his hands felt like a personal failure.

Much, he had to admit, like knowing the big boss behind the gambling ring was still at large.

Ignoring the pop in his knee and the tight muscles bunched in his neck, Brash stood and went to his whiteboards. He studied them every day, trying to make some new connection, trying to pull some new thread. The answer was here somewhere; he simply had to find it.

One board was dedicated to the fight against drugs, the other to the fight against gambling. Brash wasn't convinced the two weren't connected, but he was handling them as separate entities.

For now, the gambling board was his primary focus. He looked it over with a sharp eye. What was he missing?

The games didn't just pop up at random. They were planned, they were staged, and they were carefully orchestrated. Unfortunately, the law was always one step behind the action. The ever-changing games would come and go by the time the law showed up. Brash was confident that would eventually change. The migrant nature of illegal activity meant organizers had to depend on word of mouth to broadcast the next time and location. Word of mouth was never dependable. Soon, someone would slip up. And when they did, he planned to be there.

After ten minutes of seeing nothing new, Brash returned to his desk. He took out a file and studied the names inside. He kept a list of every person known to have some connection to gambling, no matter how small or trivial their involvement. He included innocent weekly games, even those his own family and friends attended. Their names were on his lists, too.

He kept another list of names for anyone known to attend or bet on cockfights. Whether he liked it or not, he had

Maddy to thank for some of those names. Last year, she and Genny spied on a fight, to clear her client's name of murder charges. He had ranted at the time, railing at her against the dangers and stupidity of such a stunt, but he had to admit, she had been onto something.

Cross-referencing the two lists, he had underlined any name that appeared on both. If those names appeared on any of the other lists he kept—those for drugs, theft, petty crimes, etc.—they earned an additional underline.

Only a handful of names had multiple lines.

A steely smile touched his face, but it was hardly one of amusement. He was tired of sitting back and biding his time. Brash was a man of action, and sitting here, waiting for the organizers to make their next move, wasn't only passive, it was boring. With only six names on the list, it wouldn't take long to pay each person a visit. Just a friendly little reminder that he was watching them.

His smile broadened. This time, a bit of amusement slipped amid the grooves of his smile. Anticipation danced in his eyes. This ought to shake things up a bit.

Brash grabbed his cowboy hat and stuffed it onto his head. He rushed out the door and past Vina, informing her he was going out. He burst out into the day with new determination, new vigor.

Let the games begin.

4

M adison sat amid the pillows of Vanessa Hutchins' couch, wondering how long it had taken the woman to acquire such a mass volume of Christmas cheer. The stuff was everywhere.

"I've already started re-shopping," the woman said over a mug of hot chocolate. "Do you have any idea how difficult it is, trying to remember if you bought a particular gift the first time, or the second? Glory be, I would be lost without my lists!"

"I'm sure," Madison murmured, but her attention had snagged on the fireplace. She counted no less than twenty-seven snowmen crowded upon the mantel. More spilled over onto a table nearby, with several displayed on the floor beneath it. The snowman collection was small in comparison to Vanessa's Santa collection.

"And of course, I simply can't find some of the things a second time, and certainly not at Black Friday prices."

"Really? I find Black Friday to be overrated." In truth, Madison didn't partake in the madness. Not even this year, when money was in short supply.

"You have to know how to shop, dear. There's a method to the madness." She launched into a ten-minute tutorial on how to best shop for Christmas bargains, leaving her guest with a dazed expression upon her face.

Madison couldn't decide if she was fascinated or horrified. Perhaps a bit of both.

"You—You should write a how-to guide," she murmured, for lack of something appropriate to say.

"Glory be, that would defeat the whole purpose!" Vanessa claimed. "The whole idea is to outsmart the other shoppers. If everyone knew my method, I wouldn't have an ace up my sleeve!"

"Speaking of Black Friday, let's start there. Do you recall any shoppers getting particularly angry with you that day?"

Vanessa's eyes twinkled. "If you do the day right, there's always shoppers angry with you!" she boasted.

"But no particular one comes to mind? No one you recognized who may have resented you for grabbing the deal they were after?"

"Well, I do recall that Susan Dewberry and Patricia Jones were in a huff when I grabbed the last two Puff-a-Luffs."

"The junior high teachers?"

"Yes, exactly. We were both headed to the same display, you see, and Patricia was taller than I was. She had her hand on the last two dolls, but I swooped in underneath, grabbed the dolls by the legs, and made off with them!" Her dramatic play-by-play was befitting a brave rescue effort, not an underhanded shopping expedition.

"And you didn't feel guilty about taking the dolls she had her hands on?"

Vanessa stared at her in confusion, as if she suddenly didn't understand English. She blinked a time or two before offering her wide-eyed explanation. "But they were seventy percent off. Of course, I didn't feel guilty."

Let it go, Maddy, she cautioned herself. *Keep your opinions to yourself.*

"That's the only altercation you can recall that day?"

"There was also the incident over the orthopedic shoe inserts."

Madison's eyes widened. "There's a Black Friday special for shoe inserts?"

"Oh, yes. Smart retailers know to spread the specials throughout the store, not just on popular Christmas gifts. In fact, that's part of my strategy. You see—"

Breaking in, Madison said, "I'd really like to hear more about the incident you mentioned."

"Oh, yes. Well, I knew the inserts would be going on sale, and glory be, Larry wears the most popular size. They're often out of stock, so the day before, I hid two packages of inserts behind the Kotex display. I put them in the very back, so that unless there was a sudden epidemic of menstrual flooding, the display would stay full and keep the inserts hidden. What I didn't know was that they would have a Black Friday special on feminine napkins." She rolled her eyes in frustration. "Just as I rolled up to the Kotex display, I see Georgia Dewberry there."

"You mean Susan Dewberry?"

"No, her sister-in-law, Georgia. The one with four teenage daughters. I don't have to tell you, she was stocking up on those napkins, left and right. Glory be, she cleaned that shelf off all the way to the back, and there my inserts were, bare to the world! Just as I stepped up to get them, her mother spotted them and made a grab for them. I did feel kind of bad, almost knocking the older woman down, but those were my inserts!

I'm putting them in Larry's stocking. Georgia jumped all down my throat, her little boy started crying, and before long, here came Susan, still mad about the Puff-a-Luff incident. No telling what might have happened next, but I yelled out that I had found Princess Mia dolls over on the Kotex aisle, and soon the place was swarming with shoppers. I slipped away and went to find the toothpaste I had hidden in the Ben Gay display."

Left speechless, Madison could only say, "I see."

"Other than that, the most exciting thing that happened was that I saved almost fifty percent on a matching set of bra and panties. They were for me, so luckily, they weren't stolen. Would you like to see?" Vanessa leaned forward, as if to shift her clothes.

"No!" Madison didn't mean for the word to come out so forceful, but at least Vanessa sank back down into the cushions. "Let's move on. I understand you returned to town on the following Tuesday to purchase your paper?"

"I went to three different stores to find it all. I use a different paper theme every year, you see, and this year it was snowflakes."

Madison hated to admit it, but on this, she could relate. She used a different paper for each person. It first started with colors—all red packages, for instant, went to her side of the family, all green packages went to Gray's. It made finding gifts under the tree so much easier. When the twins were born, she took it one step further. Bethani had her own special paper, Blake had his. This year, she was adding papers for Brash and Megan, a fact that pleased her to no end.

"Did anything unusual happen on that day?"

"Not that I recall. It was a quick trip, over there and back."

Madison took notes, jolting when she heard the unfamiliar *HoHo, HoHo* of the cuckoo clock.

"Isn't that delightful?" Vanessa beamed. "I found a Christmas cuckoo clock at a garage sale, but glory be, it didn't work. I salvaged the Santa and every year, I have my clocksmith change it out for me."

"There's still such a thing as a clocksmith?"

"Oh, yes. I use one right over in Riverton."

"By the way, do you know Reggie and Mona Carr?"

"I know who they are, of course, but we don't travel in the same circles. Why do you ask?"

"Just curious. So, about your Bunco group…"

After visiting with Vanessa for another hour, Madison escaped with her sanity hanging by a thread. Vanessa had a story or anecdote for every question she asked. Between the stereo, the musical pillows and rugs, and the motion-activated plush, Maddy was certain she had heard every Christmas song known to man. Her head was pounding, and she still had to swing by the Carrs.

"Someone broke into my car and stole all our gifts!" Mona Carr complained. "I spent the entire day shopping in Bryan, and for what? A total waste of my time and effort!"

"And my money," her husband glared.

"Oh, hush up, Reggie. It's all covered by insurance. Except for my time!"

"It's not like you do anything all day," her husband grumbled. "Park your tush in front of the TV and watch those game shows until the kids get in."

"Right, Reggie. And dinner just magically appears on the table, and clean clothes just magically appear in the drawers. There's a little rug fairy that comes in and does the carpets, a broom fairy that sweeps the floors." She made a rude gesture to her husband's back before huffing, "Men!"

Madison wanted to make this visit as brief as possible. The hostility in the room hung thick as fog.

"I don't want to keep you, Mrs. Carr. I just wanted to know if there was anything odd or unusual about your shopping trip. Do you recall anyone staring at you, or following you, by chance?"

"Everyone stares at her," Reggie jeered. "They want to know what that funny-looking thing is on top of her shoulders!"

"Don't start with me, Reginald. Do not start with me!"

"Please, Mrs. Carr. This could be important."

"Nope, can't think of a thing. Shopped all day, stopped for takeout on the way home, left the presents in the car because Mr. Industrious over here said he would unload. But, being the lazy bum that he is, he left them till this morning. But the joke was on him, because some other lazy fool broke the window and stole them all."

"Who are you calling lazy, you boob-tube diva?"

Mona puffed her chest out like a banty rooster. "Yeah, well, who's sitting in front of it right now, huh? I'll give you one hint. Not. Me."

Insults flung back and forth while Madison scrambled to her feet with her half-finished notes. "I just need one more thing, and you can e-mail that to me," she offered hastily. "I need a copy of the items stolen."

"I've got that right here," Mona offered. "I had to make a list of all the items and their approximate value for the insurance guy."

Madison looked at it just long enough to see a clear case of fraud. Every item listed was top of the line. Half of the items were completely out of character for the Carrs. She glanced around, noting that nothing in the room was name brand. The decor was run-of-the-mill, garage-sale quality. Why on Earth would they buy gifts such as a two-hundred-dollar espresso maker, a pair of designer shoes, and a three-hundred-dollar ice chest? She could believe the basketball goal and the forty-inch flat screen television—both seemed overly fond of the 'boob tube'—but most of the other items on the list were doubtful.

"I don't suppose you have receipts?"

"Nope, left them in the sacks," she replied quickly. "And before you ask, I paid cash."

"For all of it?"

"Oh, I might have charged one or two things. But a lot of it I paid cash for, like the espresso maker and the shoes."

"She hoards her money," Reggie volunteered. "Buys tough cuts of meat and weenies, even though I budget for rib-eye steaks and pork loin."

Mona looked ready to protest, but thought better of it. Instead, she offered a sheepish shrug. "I do what I can to make every dollar count."

"Yes, well, thank you for the list. I'll be in touch if I have any other questions."

Madison couldn't leave the Carrs' quickly enough. She knew it was wrong of her, but she just couldn't work up enough sympathy to feel sorry for their loss.

"If you need me to stay, I don't mind."

Not for the first time, her grandmother made the magnanimous offer. Madison knew there was more to the gesture than merely trying to help.

"Granny, if you don't want to go to Vegas, you don't have to."

"Of course, I want to go to Vegas," her grandmother blustered. "Who doesn't want to go to Sin City? The steady chaching of all those slot machines, just waiting for my nickels. I can hold my own on roulette, but craps is where I really shine. Don't be surprised if I come back with a nice little bundle." She rubbed her heavily veined hands together in anticipation.

"But this is like the tenth time you've offered to stay. If I didn't know better, I'd say you're nervous about going away with Sticker."

"Not nervous, mind you. Just cautious. The old coot might try something slick, like tricking me into one of those drive-through weddings I've heard about."

"Granny, don't let him pressure you into doing anything you're uncomfortable with. You have the power to say no." It was a talk she often had with her daughter, but the first time she had given it to her eighty-one-year-old grandmother.

"This isn't a sex talk, is it?" her grandmother asked emphatically. "Because I was married to the man who invented sex, I'll have you know. I've forgotten more about the deed than you'll ever know, and believe me, I learned from the best. Your grandfather, God bless his soul, was—"

Madison grabbed her ears and practically screeched, "Too much information! Definitely *not* something I need to know about my grandparents!"

"I'm not worried about the old fool trying to get me into his bed. I've outwitted more than one frisky beau in my day. But I do worry he might try to make me wife number twelve, or whatever it is he's up to by now."

"I don't think you can be legally married that many times."

"Still, I don't want him tricking me into anything. I don't mind being his date for the opening ceremony. I'll enjoy the rodeo and all the shows. Don't mind meeting his kids and one or two of his ex-wives. But if he plies me with liquor and tries to put a ring on it, we have a problem."

Madison laughed at her grandmother's somber expression. "I think you may be protesting just a little too much," she teased. "Are you trying to tell me I may get a new grandfather after this weekend?"

Instead of humor, tears came to the older woman's eyes. "No one, I mean *no one*, could ever replace my Joe."

Feeling ashamed of herself for making light of her grandmother's feelings, Maddy immediately apologized. "I'm sorry, Granny, I didn't mean to upset you. Of course, no one can replace Grandpa Joe. But Granny... it's okay to love Sticker, you know. He's a good man. And he adores you."

"I had my chance for a future with him years ago, and I let it pass me by."

"It's not too late, you know. Most people never get a second chance. Maybe you shouldn't be so quick to dismiss it."

She shook her head with determination. "You know me. I like being number one, not number eight or nine or twelve."

"It bothers you, doesn't it, that he married so many other women?"

"I feel sorry for the old fool, that's all. I'm sorry he never had what Joe and I had."

"Maybe he still could," Madison suggested softly. "You know, even if you were to marry Sticker, you wouldn't be replacing Grandpa Joe. You would be... adding someone else to love."

"I could never have what I had with your grandfather. Anything less would pale in comparison. No, I won't be marrying Sticker Pierce. I might keep time with the man, but I've been a Cessna for the best years of my life. Don't reckon I'll change that now."

"Then why are you so worried about going to Vegas with him?"

"He can be a very persuasive man. Just don't want him tricking me into doing something I'll regret."

Madison bit back a smile. What she was saying was that she didn't trust herself, but Maddy wisely kept that revelation to herself. "You go, have a wonderful time, and when you get home, we'll go on a baking binge. Cookies and cakes and anything else we can freeze."

"I sure wish your parents could come for the holidays. This will be the third Christmas in a row they've missed."

"I know, but they say they can't get away right now. Too much missionary work yet to be done."

"I don't guess that boy of mine will ever settle down," Granny Bert grumbled. "Hope he finds his way clear to come to my funeral."

"Which will not be anytime soon, so there's no need to fret about it," Madison said in a firm voice. "Was there anything you needed to borrow from me? You have a jacket, right?"

"Wool coat, already packed. And a sweater."

"Do you plan to do any Christmas shopping while you're there?"

"Nah, no need to lug packages back. And you know I like to shop local whenever I can. Which reminds me. What did you find out about the Christmas Crimes?"

Propping her hands onto her trim hips, Madison accused her grandmother, "It was you, wasn't it? You're the one that tipped Dane off!"

"Your cousin is a savvy reporter, young lady. He doesn't need help from his old granny to get stories."

"I notice you didn't deny it."

"Everyone in town has already heard about the robberies. Vanessa Hutchins has the loosest lips in town. She couldn't keep a secret if you sewed it into her inside gums."

"What about Reggie and Mona Carr? I had the displeasure of meeting them today."

"Poor you. They haven't lived here all that long. Five or six years, at the most. One of those transplants from the city, eager to move to the freedom of the country, then want to bring all their rules and regulations of city living with them. Tried to stir up all kinds of trouble while I was mayor."

"I can certainly see that. Being in their living room was like being in a war zone."

"Serves them right to get a little payback karma."

"Except they're lying to their insurance company about what was stolen."

"How so?"

"Do you really think they would buy a top-of-the-line espresso machine? I saw a knock-off coffee maker on their counter. And a Yeti cooler? Please."

"Speaking of gifts… you're going to do the shopping for the Angel Tree, right? You and the twins are taking care of that while I'm in Vegas."

"Yes, Granny. For the umpteenth time, I'm taking care of everything. The donation boxes have been emptied at least a dozen times. It was sweet of you to put them at all your grandchildren's businesses, trying to bring us more traffic. Plus, at Genny's restaurant, of course."

Granny Bert brushed off the praise, concentrating instead on the last of her statement. "She might not be blood kin, but she might as well be."

"I think the kids sometimes forget she's not their actual aunt. The other day, I heard Bethani claim she got her blue eyes from her Aunt Genny!" Madison laughed. "Anyway, donations are going great. I'll use the money collected to finish shopping this week and we'll be ready for the Christmas parade, right on schedule."

"Don't get so busy with your detective work that you forget."

"Don't worry, I'm on it. Before you leave, though … what can you tell me about the illegal gambling game in town? Brash is running himself ragged, trying to chase them down."

"My inside track has gone cold," Granny Bert said in disgust, shaking her gray head. "Whatever is happening, they're laying low. I can't find out a thing. But I suspect it means there's something big coming up. I feel a storm a-brewin'."

Madison nibbled on her lower lip. "That's what Brash said. I'm worried, Granny. I'm afraid he may get hurt."

"Brash is a big boy and a fine lawman. He can take care of himself. The best thing you can do is stay out of his way and not distract him. Let him focus on his job and get this taken care of, once and for all."

"I'll try. Oh, there's the doorbell. Looks like your date is here."

Her grandmother peeked from the curtain and saw Sticker Pierce waiting patiently on her porch. He wore his own line of western wear, from his custom-tooled boots to his carefully creased cowboy hat. With his monogrammed shirt, starched jeans, and oversized championship belt buckle, he cut quite the figure, even for a man his age.

"Well, butter my buns and call me a biscuit!" Granny Bert whistled. "That man still knows how to fill out a pair of jeans."

"Granny Bert!"

Her grandmother gave her a thumb's up. "Don't worry, girl. I'll keep my virtue—and my name—intact. You handle the angel tree; I'll handle the devil in blue jeans."

5

Two days later, Madison wondered how things had gone so terribly wrong. What would Granny Bert say when she heard about *this*?

It began as an ordinary day. After getting the kids off to school, Madison ran errands for a few of her clients, took care of some phone calls, and did the laundry. By the time the twins got home, she had their shopping list sorted and prioritized.

Even though Granny Bert favored shopping local, Madison knew she could get more for her money in Bryan-College Station. It was an hour away, but had the nearest shopping mall and big box stores, as well as a variety of specialty shops, three Wal-Marts, and more restaurants than Blake could ever eat his way through, no matter how hard he tried.

The Angel Tree had an alarming number of needy children this year, and fewer benefactors than usual. It broke Madison's heart to think there might be disillusioned children on Christmas morning. Along with the money collected for the Angel Tree, she and the twins were donating a portion of their meager budget to brighten the lives of some of those less fortunate.

She asked Blake to supervise the athletic needs of the children on their list. He knew more about what sport enthusiasts wanted. Bethani took care of fashion needs and little girl toys. Madison added the practical side of the gifts—warm socks, jackets, and feel-good throws and pillows. By the time they finished shopping, her car was so full that she allowed Blake to catch a ride home with friends they saw in the mall.

"At the risk of sounding like my twin, Mr. Garbage Disposal, I'm hungry," Bethani announced.

"We ate dinner!"

"That was like three hours ago. Can we stop and get something to eat? Please?"

"What about your brother?"

"What about him? If he gets home before us, he's a big boy, he has a key. But if I know him, he'll con Mrs. Baines into stopping somewhere, too. Oh, can we stop at *Tasty's*?" Bethani asked eagerly. "They have awesome cheddar fries!"

"I've heard a lot about them, but I haven't tried them yet."

"Momma Matt took us by there the other day. You have to try the Caramel Crazy Latte. It's like super delish!"

Laughing at her daughter's enthusiasm, Madison agreed to try the new restaurant. Handily situated on their way of town, it also stayed open late. *Good thing*, she thought, since many other places were already closed. Bethani confirmed the fact by checking on her phone. She liked the place so well, she downloaded their app after visiting the first time.

Five minutes later, they saw the line at the drive-through window. "Are you sure you want to eat here?"

"Yes, Mom, it is crazy good. Trust me. It's worth the wait."

"It better be. It's almost an hour drive home and you have school tomorrow, young lady."

"I could skip," the teen offered innocently. "You know, stay home and wrap all these gifts we bought, that kind of thing."

"How generous of you, Beth."

Bethani ignored the sarcasm in her mother's voice. "Just doing my part for mankind." She flashed an innocent smile so charming, for a moment, it reminded Madison of Genny.

Maybe we're blood-kin, after all, she mused. *But no, that smile actually looked more like her father's. Back when Gray smiled all the time. Back before...*

Madison shook herself from her reverie. She didn't want to go there, not tonight. Her capricious teenager was in a good mood right now, and she wanted to enjoy every moment of it. With the hormonal tidal waves of a sixteen-year-old girl, that could change at any moment.

"I was proud of you and Blake today, babe. I know some of that was your own money, and you freely spent it on others. That shows not only maturity, but generosity and compassion."

"It felt good today, you know, buying gifts for all those kids. I know I don't always show it, but I know how fortunate Blake and I are. Not just because we have the Big House and all our stuff, but... you know. Because of family, and all that."

Madison's eyes misted with emotion. "Yes, Beth, we're fortunate, indeed," she agreed softly.

Rolling up to the menu board, they placed their order and patiently sat in the pick-up line. "At least the line is moving fairly quickly," Madison said.

The teen slid her mother a sly glance. "No hurry, since I'm not going to school tomorrow."

"Nice try, no cigar. I never agreed to your generous offer, my dear."

While they waited for their food, they discussed some of their better buys of the day. When they reached the window to collect their food, Bethani was still laughing about the spectacle her brother made while trying to squeeze a particularly large box into the backseat. The young woman at the window overheard enough of the story to lean out and peer into the over-stuffed backseat.

"Wow, I bet that was tough getting in there! Let me guess," she grinned. "Christmas shopping?" She had vivid pink streaks in her hair that matched her nail polish.

"For the Angel Tree!" Bethani volunteered jovially from across the car, leaning low to share her smile.

"Ah, that's nice. Giving to others."

"We do what we can," Madison smiled as she accepted the bag of food. "Mmm, smells great. Did you include straws?"

"There should be some inside, but here you go, just in case."

"Okay, thanks!"

Bethani leaned back down. "Merry Christmas!"

As they pulled back onto the highway, Madison asked, "Did you know that girl?"

"I think I've seen her around before. Someone said Addison's cousin worked here. Maybe that's her, I don't know." The teen shrugged as she pulled out her cheesy fries. "I was just being friendly. Here, try one of these and tell me they aren't the best you've ever tasted!"

It was a rare treat to share time alone with her daughter, so Madison took full advantage. She kept the conversation light and playful. They discussed what cookies they would make when Granny Bert came home, sang along with the Christmas carols on CD, and laughed all the way back to River County.

The laughter died a few miles before they reached Juliet.

"Mom, I think that's a cop. He's flashing his lights at you."

Madison looked into her rear-view mirror and saw a car quickly approaching, flashing its lights. Something about the overhead bar looked wrong. "Those aren't cop lights, are they?"

"I don't know, but he definitely wants you to stop!"

"I'm not stopping just because someone flashes their lights at me. It could be a scam. Haven't you heard about those girls that were kidnapped? They pulled over on a deserted road, much like this one, for what they thought was a patrolman. Turned out to be a pervert."

Panic rose in Bethani's voice. "Then what are we going to do? He's gaining on us. He might try to shoot out the tires or something!"

"He's not going to shoot out the tires!" she snapped, hoping she sounded more confident than she felt. What would she do if he did? Could she control the car at this speed? Reluctantly, Madison eased off the accelerator. "Scroll down to Brash's number. Don't call him yet, but have it ready to press if I tell you to."

"Mom, I'm scared."

"There's no need to be scared. I'm not stopping until I know it's legit. And if it is legit, I haven't done anything wrong."

"Except refuse to stop!"

"We'll cross that bridge when we get there." As the car came up alongside her, she added, "Which could be any moment now."

For a moment, Madison feared the car would edge her off the road. Then she saw the emblem on the side, identifying it as part of the state wildlife department.

Relief flooded through her, weakening her knees. "Oh, thank goodness. It's a game warden."

"What do they want with us?" Bethani cried.

"I don't know, but they want us to pull over." She found a safe place to pull onto the shoulder and eased the car to a stop. The game warden pulled in directly behind her, his bright lights blinding them. All Madison could see was a man's silhouette approaching her stopped vehicle.

Rolling down the window, she asked, "Is something wrong, officer?" She wasn't sure it was the right title, but it never hurt to flatter someone wearing a badge.

It struck her as odd that the man's hair was as long as it was. Most men on the state payroll wore neatly cropped hair and clean-shaven faces. If they did have a beard, they were always neat and properly groomed. This man's shaggy beard and long hair were the first things Madison noticed.

The second thing she noticed was that he kept his head bent, so that his ranger-style hat shadowed his face. Which was the third oddity. Where was his customary cowboy hat? And unlike most law enforcement authorities, his clothes were ill fitting and wrinkled.

Madison got an uneasy feeling, even before he spoke.

"I need to search your car," he said without preamble.

"Ex*cuse* me?"

"Said I need to search your car. We had reports of a car matching this description carrying illegal hides across county lines. You'll have to get out of the car."

She heard Bethani sputtering in the seat beside her, but Madison motioned for her to be quiet. She offered the man her best smile. "As I think you can see, there's not an extra bit of space in this car. We don't have room for any hides in here!" She forced a laugh, but the man didn't share her humor.

"Could be hidden beneath all the junk."

"Junk? Those are Christmas gifts for the Angel Tree!"

"Don't matter. Gotta search your car. Now step out."

His lack of manners and his grammar were the final clues. Officers of the law, particularly those in the South, were polite and referred to women with the respectful title of 'ma'am.' This man was definitely a fraud.

"I don't believe I will," Madison said. She heard Bethani gasp in surprise. Very subtly, Maddy raised her hand to her face and pretended to smooth back her hair. She hoped that Bethani saw the position of her thumb and little finger, in the universal sign of 'call me.' Or, in this case, 'call Brash.' She sent the teen a pointed look, sweeping her gaze down to the phone in her hands. A tiny flick of her head warned her to hide the device.

"I'd like to see your warrant, please," Madison continued. She leaned forward just enough to shield Bethani from the man's view. From the corner of her eye, she saw her daughter slip the phone out of sight as she pressed a button.

"Don't need a warrant," the man claimed. "Have probable cause. For a game warden, that's all that's needed."

Madison vaguely remembered reading something to that effect while working with a client on a property dispute. They had investigated a variety of options, including calling in the wildlife department for alleged poaching.

She tried stalling. "What kind of hides are you looking for?"

Her resistance surprised the man, but he was quick to answer, "Coon hides."

Madison used her haughtiest expression, one she hoped mimicked her mother-in-law. "Seriously, do I *look* like someone who hunts raccoons?"

"You might not hunt 'em. You might be trying to sell 'em. Same difference. Now get out while I search your vehicle."

"I will do no such thing!"

A radio crackled at his waist, and Madison had her first hint of doubt. What if he were a true game warden? A rude one, but legally certified? Was she breaking the law by refusing him?

"Look, lady, don't make this harder on yourself. I can have the sheriff here in five minutes. He'll arrest you, of course, but I can call him if you want."

She briefly considered mentioning Brash's name, but she discarded the thought immediately. She refused to take advantage of her relationship with him, even if he was a special investigator with the county. Besides, he was probably already on his way.

"I'll tell you what. I'll allow you to search my car, but only if I can remain inside, and only if you go ahead and make that call."

"Mom!"

She brushed Bethani's protest aside. Knowing Brash was on his way gave her a confidence she didn't feel.

The game warden shrugged his thin shoulders. "Up to you, lady. I'll make that call and you can unlock the car. Start with the trunk."

He stepped to the back of her car and she heard him talking, presumably calling for an officer. If nothing else, her license number would go out over the air, dispatch would hear it, and alert Brash. Hoping she had made the right choice, Madison pressed the remote button for the trunk.

"Mom!" Bethani hissed. "Mr. de didn't pick up!"

Refusing to panic, Madison tried to remain calm. "Send him a text. The game warden is at the back of the car and won't see you."

Her blue eyes wide, Bethani said, "Mom, I don't think he's a real game warden."

"Neither do I," Madison admitted. "Tell Brash where we are and tag it 9-1-1 so he'll know it's an emergency. Send it to Cutter, too. I'll try to reach my phone and call 9-1-1 in earnest."

The teen looked at her phone. "I don't have any service!"

They kept trying to get a message out, until the uniformed man came back to the window. Both quickly slid their phones out of sight.

"See, I told you I didn't have any hides," Maddy said. "Now may we go?"

"Not until I search the backseat. I'll make it quick."

He jerked open the door and removed her purchases. With the lights from his car still blinding her, Madison couldn't see where he put the presents. "Please don't damage my purchases. As I said, they are for the Angel Tree in The Sisters."

"Oh, I aim to take real good care of your purchases, lady." When he grinned, she saw his decaying teeth, a definite hint that he used meth.

After just a few minutes, he had the backseat empty. He stood back as he slammed the door. "Well, looks like you were right. Don't see any hides in there, after all. You're free to go."

"What? Not without my purchases, I'm not!"

"Oh, we gotta keep those as evidence," he grinned. "Book 'em into... into evidence." He grappled for a more official-sounding term and came up short.

"I don't think so!" Maddy stormed. "I demand you give me my gifts back!"

"I don't think you're in a position to demand a thing, missy, but I'll see what the sheriff has to say." He turned on his heel and she saw his silhouette retreating against the bright lights as he walked back to his car. She thought she saw a door open.

Before she knew what was happening, the car spun out and made a U-turn in the middle of the highway, racing off in the other direction.

"Mom, he left!" Bethani screeched. "Where are all our things?"

With a sinking feeling, Madison opened her door to peer into the night. Using the light of her cell phone, she got out and circled around the car. She returned with her lower lip trembling.

"Beth," she whispered, breathlessly. She soon found her voice and blurted out, "We've been robbed!"

With no cell service, Madison knew she had to drive into town to report the robbery. She marked the spot by tying the bag from *Tasty's* on a nearby bush, then drove as fast as she could to the police station. Brash wasn't on duty, but she gave her statement to Officer Schimanski.

By the time she was finished with her initial report, Brash arrived.

"Oh, Brash, I feel so foolish!" was the first thing she said.

"Foolish? You are a victim, Maddy! That man falsely impersonated an officer of the law."

"But I *knew* he wasn't legit. We both did!" She made frantic hand motions as she described the discrepancies. "His speech was wrong, he didn't call me ma'am, his hair was long and needed a cut. He—He had a long, shaggy beard, but the more I think about it, I think it was fake. It looked just like those on that show you like to watch."

"*Duck Dynasty?*"

"Yes, yes. Just like that. But it was the wrong color for his complexion, and—and the whole thing was just a set-up, and I fell for it!" she wailed.

Brash gathered her into his arms. He reached out and included Bethani in the embrace. "It doesn't sound like you did, sweetheart. It sounds like you knew he was a fraud and that you did just the right thing. Bethani was smart to hide her phone and try to make the call. I got the message about two minutes ago," he smiled ruefully. "But she put all the right things in it, so good girl, Beth." He gave her a warm wink and a quick squeeze. "And you did the right thing by refusing to get out of the car and demanding that he call the sheriff. If he had been legit, the sheriff would have understood a woman's reluctance to leave her car in a situation such as that."

"When—When he didn't call me 'ma'am,' I knew he was a fraud."

Brash smiled. "That speaks well for the state of Texas and law officers everywhere."

"I can give you a description, Brash. He was about five feet ten, and very thin. He had dirty blond hair and—"

"I have a picture of him," Bethani announced. She wiggled out of Brash's arms and pulled her phone from her back pocket. "Mom's hair is in the way on this one." She swiped the screen for the next image. "And there's her nose. But there! There's the guy!"

"Good work, honey! And smart thinking!" Brash hugged the teen, who couldn't help but glow from his praise.

Bethani broke out in unexpected laughter. "You should have heard Mom! She looked down her nose at the man and spoke to him like she was some sort of diva or something. 'Seriously, do I *look* like someone who hunts raccoons?' It was hilarious!" She doubled over in mirth as she impersonated her mother.

Nerves made the situation seem funnier than it actually was. It took both women several minutes to quieten down and sober. Once they did, reality came crashing back in.

"We lost all the gifts, Brash!" Madison wailed in misery. "The presents for the Angel Tree. He must have had someone with him, loading the packages as he took them out. The lights were too bright for me to see a thing. We spent the entire afternoon shopping, and now they're gone. Just gone! Just like Vanessa Hutchins and those Carr people." A new thought occurred to her, and a look of horror crossed her face. She slapped her hands to her mouth. "Granny Bert," she moaned. "How will I ever explain this to Granny Bert?"

After taking Madison and Bethani home and staying with them until they were settled and calm, Brash returned to the office. He studied the photo Bethani had taken with her cell phone. It wasn't the best of pictures, but it showed enough for him to make a tentative identification. Unless he was badly mistaken, that was Dickey Fowler in that wrinkled game warden suit.

Pulling out his trusty lists of names, he scanned over them for the name. There it was, Dickey Fowler, underlined three times. Once for petty theft, once for assault and battery, once for drug possession. Only two of the charges had stuck, landing him in the River County Jail for dual visits.

He searched his memory banks for what he knew about the man. He lived just out of town in a rundown shack a few years past inhabitable for decent folk, yet suitable for riffraff like Fowler. Brash doubted the shack even had indoor plumbing. If he was right, the twenty-something-year-old was kin to Bernie Havlicek in a roundabout way. He would make a call to his mother for the specifics. She didn't know the town's history as well as Granny Bert, but she was a close second.

In the meantime, Vina could pull up the official records. Between the two, he would have a better idea of how Dickey Fowler fit into all this.

One thing was for certain. Tonight had been no coincidence.

At best, it was the latest Christmas crime, an alarming situation that was quickly escalating.

At worst, it was a warning. He had been sniffing around, asking questions, letting folks know he was watching. Targeting Madison may have been their response: he was getting too close.

6

"It could happen to anyone, child," her grandmother said over the telephone. "Don't beat yourself up over it."

"But I promised you, Granny Bert! I said, 'I got this,' and I thought I did. I really did. I thought you were being overly pessimistic, thinking I couldn't handle it. But it turned out you were right," Madison moaned miserably.

"I knew you could handle it, girl, or I would never have left it in your capable hands."

"Capable? I let someone steal the presents from me, right out from under my nose!"

"What choice did you have? You were right to do what you did. Gifts can be replaced, you and Bethani can't."

"I know, but the whole thing was a set-up. It just irks me, knowing I was a part of a scam." She seethed for a moment, before adding, "Oh, and did I tell you? This has actually happened before. The call went to the county sheriff, so Brash didn't hear about it at first. But when he started asking around, he found out that a couple of days ago, someone stopped to help a stranded motorist, and while they were fixing a flat tire, someone stole all their packages. Right here, on this very road!"

"Shall I point out that if all of you had shopped local, this sort of thing wouldn't have happened?" Granny Bert harrumphed.

Madison groaned aloud. She knew she was getting off too easy. Now she would have to hear a lecture about supporting the local economy.

"How can you expect our small-town stores to stay in business if you run off to Bryan or Waco or Houston shopping all the time? You spend your money in the big city, you support the big city. You spend your money local, you support your friends and neighbors. You could have bought most every single gift right there in Juliet and Naomi, instead of traveling an hour away to throw your money at some big corporation that knows diddly-squat when it comes to customer service!"

"I know, but—"

"But nothing! When my washing machine went out last week, who came to my rescue? *Evans Hardware*, that's who. If I had bought it from one of those big box stores, they would have dug around in their computers, decided my warranty was up unless I wanted to pay a small fortune to upgrade it for two years, then they would have either sent a repairman one day next week—sometime between the hours of noon and five, like I didn't have a life and had nothing better to do than sit around waiting all day—or else they would have sold me a new one, gone back into their computers to locate the nearest one, tried to sell me another extended warranty, and promise delivery by a week from Lord knows when! Again, between the hours of noon till five!" She paused only long enough to draw in a breath. "But no. I was smart and bought my machine locally, so when I called them up, they had someone out that very afternoon to look at it. And in the meantime, while my clothes were soaking in all that bleach because Blake spilled grape juice all over my tablecloth, Betty Sue Evans came over, helped me wring the clothes dry, and took them to her house to finish washing. Now that, my girl, is customer service!"

Madison hung her head and listened to her grandmother rant. At the first opportunity, she broke in, "Yes, I understand, and you do have a point. But I was spending donated money, Granny, and I felt it was my responsibility to get the most bang for the buck. The fact is, I can find better buys in the bigger towns."

"Bang for the buck? That money was donated by local folks, to benefit local kids! The least you could have done was spend it local! Did it ever occur to you that most of those kids' parents work at our local stores? They can't afford to travel back and forth to work in Bryan every day, so they work right there in town, where their jobs depend on their friends and neighbors to support them. Keeping the local stores in business means keeping local jobs. Talk about bang for your buck!"

Duly chastised, Madison could do nothing but agree. "You're right. You are absolutely right. And when I re-buy the presents, I promise I will buy them right here in The Sisters." *I'll pay twice as much, but I will buy them here.*

"Darn tootin' you will, because Sticker and I are footing the bill to do just that!"

Madison bit back a smile, hearing their names linked together so casually. "So how are things going there, Granny? Are you having fun?"

"A bit noisy for my tastes, but the food's good. So is the gambling. I raked in five hundred dollars on a penny machine yesterday. I'm setting that aside for the Angel Tree."

"And Sticker? How was the ceremony?"

"I told you, child, I'm not marrying that old coot!" her grandmother snapped.

"I meant the opening ceremony, Granny. Wasn't that why you went out there in the first place? For him to be honored at the National Finals Rodeo?"

"Oh, that. It was fine, fine. Lots of pomp and circumstance, bright lights, and flashy women. Right up the old fool's alley. Cutter and Genny were here, you know. Didn't they tell you about it?"

"I haven't had a chance to talk to her yet. Say. You don't think they'll have one of those quickie Las Vegas weddings, do you?" she cried in dismay.

"You sound upset. If you ask me, that's the best way to go. No muss, no fuss. People spend a fortune on weddings these days."

Before her grandmother could go off on another tangent, Madison explained, "I know, but Genny deserves something special. I'm looking forward to helping her plan the wedding of her dreams, just like she did for me when I got married. She's waited a long time for this, you know."

"She was waiting for the right man, not the flashy wedding. Judging by the stars in both their eyes, they couldn't care less about the ceremony itself. It's the wedding night they're after."

Not wanting to get into *that* conversation again, Madison said, "Look, Granny, I have to go. You be safe and have a good time. Don't worry about things here. I promise, I won't let you down again."

"You didn't let me down the first time," her grandmother said. "I'll be home day after tomorrow. Have my baking pans ready."

"Will do!"

Madison hung up the phone, still smiling. Her grandmother was a handful, that was for sure.

"I've been thinking."

Blake made the announcement as the credits from the movie rolled. They were watching *Home Alone*, another oldie-but-goldie in their Christmas collection.

"Well, this is a first!" his sister quipped. "Better watch out."

"I'm serious. I've been giving it some thought, and I think we need to start a new Christmas tradition this year."

"What did you have in mind?" Madison asked. Knowing her son, it revolved around food.

A scowl puckered the boy's handsome face. "That's just it, I'm not sure. I just think we need to start something new. You know, because this year we're starting over. New house, new town, new friends." He shrugged, suddenly embarrassed by his sentimental observation.

Touched by his thoughtfulness, Madison smiled. "I think that is an excellent idea, Blake."

"We can keep all the old ones," he was quick to note. "But maybe we could add something new. Something that's just ours. Without…" He stopped suddenly, uncomfortable in finishing his thought.

"Without Mr. de?" his sister was quick to smirk.

"No, I didn't mean him. Maybe we could even include him."

Bethani rolled her eyes. "You're just suffering from hero worship. Ever since he took you hunting and you killed that big buck, you're like the president of the Brash deCordova fan club!"

They bickered for a few moments before Madison broke in, her voice gentle. "Were you referring to Genny, Blake? I know you love her, but it's okay if her being here bothers you. It's only until she and Cutter get married, but I guess I volunteered our home without consulting you two." Realizing that fact in retrospect, Madison frowned at her oversight. "I'm sorry. I should have asked you both before I offered our house to her."

"You moron!" Bethani accused, tossing a pillow at her twin. "How selfish can you be, wanting to turn Aunt Genny out on the streets! And after the way she spoils you, cooking all your favorite foods!"

He easily deflected the second pillow. "Hey, knock it off! I wasn't talking about Aunt Genny. She and Cutter can both move in, for all I care. And if you hadn't suggested it, Mom, we would have."

His mother looked relieved. "Okay, good. Because sometimes I forget that you two are growing up so quickly, and that you should have a voice in family decisions."

"Yeah, that's kind of what I'm getting at. All our old traditions are great and all, but... but they're ones you and Dad started, when Beth and I were little." A brief look of pain crossed his face. "But Dad's gone now. And maybe... maybe it's time we started something new, that's just ours. Without... without him."

Bethani sniffed, but for once, she had no snide comeback. Maddy blinked her dewy eyes and offered a shaky smile. "I think that is a really good idea, sweetie. You're right. Moving here to The Sisters, making new friends and a new life for ourselves, in this fabulous new home, deserves a new tradition!" She swiped away a rogue tear that escaped her lashes. "So, what will it be? Let's decide together!"

"You know, I really enjoyed shopping for the Angel Tree," Blake said. "I know it didn't end up like we thought, but that was cool, pitching in to help like that. Maybe that could be something."

His generosity made Madison proud. "Excellent suggestion."

"You know how we bake cookies for all the mothers on Mother's Day? Maybe we could do that. Give cookies to the needy, or something," Bethani suggested.

Blake vigorously nodded his blond head. "And that night we lit the house. That was cool, inviting the neighbors in for hot cocoa and cookies."

"But we can't do that all the time," his twin cautioned. "Do you know how many people drive by every night, just to look at our house? We'd have a revolving door!"

"No, but maybe we could find a way to take the cookies out to them," Madison said. She wasn't keen on the idea of inviting strangers into her home, but this was Christmas, the season of giving. A gesture of kindness might not change someone's life, but it could certainly change their day.

"Hey, I could rig something up!" Blake said, his blue eyes glowing with excitement. "Not exactly an app, but some sort of text program. We could have a sign in the yard to text a certain number, and, if we're home, we could take a bag of cookies out to their car!"

"And if we're not home, or we've run out of cookies, we could have a recording of a Christmas song or a poem or something!"

The ideas swirled, some more outrageous than others. For Maddy, the best part was the excitement shining in the twins' eyes, and the laughter that rent the air. She could imagine nothing sweeter, not even the cookies that they planned.

"So, we'll get to work on the details, and see if it's do-able," she summarized after a half hour of brainstorming.

"This is going to be fun! I know Aunt Genny and Granny Bert and Megan will help us do the baking."

"Jamil's dad is a computer programmer. He'll help me with the text system."

"As cool as this one is, I was thinking we might also like to add another tradition," Madison suggested.

"Like what?"

"What if we hosted a big Christmas meal here, for our closest family and friends? I know we will already be spending time with them, but when we do Christmas at Granny Bert's, it's with the entire family. Between all the aunts, uncles, and cousins, there's like fifty of us. Genny will probably spend a lot of time with the Montgomerys this year, and your friends will be with their families. The deCordovas have invited us to come there on Christmas Eve, but again, that's a big bunch." Seeing Bethani's sharp look, she was quick to assure her, "I haven't given them an answer yet, not without talking to you two. But I was thinking maybe Christmas evening, after everyone has done their own presents and had time with their own families, we could invite our closest family here, and exchange presents among ourselves. Maybe serve something totally un-Christmassy, like Mexican food or something."

"As much as I love turkey and dressing, we have it like four times in a row," Blake agreed.

"I like that idea," Bethani said. "Like stretching the day out, as long as we can."

"Yeah, after opening gifts on Christmas morning, the afternoon is usually a bummer," her brother agreed.

Bethani gave a smart nod. "Then it's official. We'll be saving the best until last."

Madison sat back with a smile on her face. This was new, hearing the twins take charge and make plans for the holidays, but it was nice. Like it or not, her babies were quickly growing up, and it was important they have a voice in family events. Helping with the planning gave the teens a personal interest and ensured their participation. Madison firmly believed that cultivating family traditions was one of the most important things she could do as a parent.

Roots, she believed, were vital to all living things. Particularly to families.

7

"**B**ad weeds," Brash grumbled, reading over the reports he held in his hands. "Someone ought to pull up the Fowler family roots and spray 'em with weed poisoning. Nothing but trouble, the whole bunch of them."

What the police reports couldn't tell him about Dickey Fowler, Lydia deCordova could. For double measure, he called Granny Bert's cell phone. On her way home from the airport, she confirmed the worst of it.

"Lowlife thugs," she all but spat. "Product of inbreeding. While Dickey, Sr. was down in Huntsville on death row for killin' their neighbor—some scuttle over a pet rooster, I think it was—his momma Lois got pregnant by her father-in-law. She named the baby Dickey, Jr., but he's Harlan Fowler's child, no doubt."

"While that is disgusting, it's not exactly inbreeding," Brash said.

"It is when Harlan is Lois' uncle. And it goes back further than that. Lois' grandparents were second cousins."

"I feel like I need a shower," Brash muttered.

"The only decent one out of the whole lot was Billy, Lois' brother. He moved off and became a game warden for the state, but he was killed a few years back in a freak accident, trying to untangle two fighting bucks from going over a waterfall. Somehow, his sleeve got caught up in their horns, and the whole lot of them drowned. A darned shame, since he was the only one with a lick of sense and decency."

"I remember reading about that. Didn't realize the man was from here."

"He distanced himself from the family, and who can blame him? He named his sister as beneficiary in his will, though, so when he died, they sent his last effects home to her."

That explained the uniform.

"She took the insurance money and went to Louisiana gambling, instead of fixing up her house like she should have done. Have you seen that dump Dickey Jr. lives in? The utilities were cut off three years ago when Lois died, but he was too lazy to move out. That place is going to fall in around him one of these days."

"I was thinking he was related in some way to Bernie Havlicek."

"Sure is. Dickey Fowler's grandmother was a Havlicek, which makes him third cousins to Bernie Havlicek."

Bernie Havlicek's name was on every list Brash kept, and underlined multiple times. He was known as a troublemaker and small-time criminal. Even though his name came up in various investigations and he was a POI in half the crimes committed within the area, he somehow managed to skirt the law, evading arrest on mere technicalities. Brash had visited him two days ago, letting him know he had eyes on him.

It could be no coincidence that Maddy was targeted.

"You're right," Brash ground out. "A family of lowlifes."

Calling Dickey Fowler's habitat a 'house' was an insult to structures everywhere, Brash decided. He approached the residence on foot. No need to announce his visit and give the man time to run.

Going in on foot meant leaving his cruiser three hundred yards away, out by the dirt-paved county road. It meant weaving his way through the overgrown woods and weeds threatening to overtake the property. A pitted gravel road led straight up to the house, but Brash chose to stick to the tree line, where his advance would be less noticeable.

Fifty yards out, he could smell the outhouse. It was the rickety lean-to to the left of the old home place. Both structures looked like a stiff wind could lay them out flat. With any luck, a norther would blow in this afternoon and do the world a favor. Flies buzzed around the outhouse, making almost as much racket as the coon dog tied nearby.

So much for a stealthy approach.

The coon dog bayed out a warning that a stranger was near. Brash spoke to the dog in low, calm tones, but the dog continued its protest, racing up and down its drag chain as it strained to be free. From the looks of it, the canine was one meal away from starvation. Brash made a mental note to call Animal Welfare.

Edging his way around the side of the house, keeping well away from the reach of the dog, Brash peered into the nearest window. Between the grime and the grease and the condensation, his vision was limited, but there was no missing the collapsed ceiling in the middle of the room.

How did a person live in a dump like that? He cringed with the thought of it as he continued around the back of the house. The lower half of one window sported a cardboard panel in lieu of glass; another was riddled with cracks and dings, all centered around a distinct bullet hole. The house was built upon blocks, but Brash swore he could take it down with one swift kick. The two pilings he could see were crumbling, and both were an inch or two off kilter. The pathetic floor that spanned between them sagged enough to make the third window a handy height for spying.

Through the grungy panes, he saw what must be the living area of the house. It looked more like the aftermath of a tornado. Crumbled newspapers, empty take-out bags, discarded clothes, and all manners of filth scattered about the room. Amid the trash, he could see a broken-down sofa, an old Formica-topped table, two chairs with ripped and gutted cushions, a box fan, and the barest bones of a kitchen. More flies buzzed around the over-flowing trash can, where pizza boxes and beer cans flourished.

With a grunt, Brash noted the one item of luxury in the otherwise desolate room. A fifty-inch flat screen television sat on the floor across from the couch, powered by an extension cord. The house might lack indoor plumbing, but it had electricity.

There was one more room on the far end of the house. The back window was covered with what looked like an Indian blanket, so he eased his way to the end. The window there had a tattered set of old louvered blinds, most of the slats broken or bent. Brash peered through the gaps and viewed the sorry excuse of a bedroom. It looked as if someone had begun packing up the house. Assorted items—framed pictures, a lamp, a broken mirror, old linens—spilled from opened cardboard boxes. Bulging trash bags piled upon one another in one corner. A stack of old magazines made a leaning tower beside a cluttered chest of drawers. Somewhere under a jumble of dirty sheets and soiled laundry was an old mattress attached to a rusty iron bedstead. In an antique store, the bed would be valuable. In this dump, it was most likely contaminated.

Seeing no sign of Dickey in any of the rooms, Brash proceeded to the front door. The handle didn't work, so all it took was a firm knock to push the door inward.

"Dickey Fowler?" he asked, knocking a second time. "Dickey Fowler, this is Police Chief Brash deCordova. May I come in?"

The house was empty. After a brief round through the rooms, Brash hurried out for a breath of fresh air. Judging from the box of chicken wings that had yet to grow a bacteria beard—as opposed to the leftover pizza, tacos, and fried chicken all sporting mold and fuzz—Dickey had been here recently. Brash saw none of Maddy's purchases in the house, but he did see the crumpled uniform of a state game warden thrown haphazardly over the couch. He snapped off pictures of it and other items of interest, but left everything untouched.

Making another sweep around the perimeter of the sad shack, he again noted the heavy-duty extension cord that fed into the bedroom window by way of the broken windowpane.

"Surely not," Brash muttered. His eyes traced the thick cord strung across the yard before it disappeared into the woods. He looked around and spotted the power pole on the property. There was a gaping hole in the electrical box, right where the meter should be. "That sorry son of a—"

Brash's words faded away as he followed the cord into the woods, where it connected to another cord. A cluster of trees, a broken barbed wire fence, and two extension cords later, he came to the neighbor's power pole. The cords were feeding directly off their meter.

Nostrils flared in anger, Brash marched into the neatly kept yard he knew belonged to Gus and Joan Prather. He rapped on the door and waited for someone to answer. In contrast to the shack on the other side of the trees, the Prathers' older mobile home was neat and tidy, and in good repair. It was dressed for the holidays, a string of colorful lights draped along the roof and over the rails of the front porch where he stood.

"Why, Officer de, I didn't hear you drive up!" the older woman said in greeting, wringing her wet hands on a dishtowel. "Come in, come in. Can I get you something to drink? Coffee? Sweet tea?"

Brash stepped into the dimly lit room, noticing that most of the lights were off in other areas of the house.

"A bit dark in here, Miss Joan. How do you see to do your sewing?" Joan Prather was best known as the local seamstress, offering a wide range of services that included sewing, alterations, and mending. She did the work from her home, as evidenced by the sewing machine set up near the front window, immediately next to the Christmas tree.

"I open the curtains when I work, and I have a lamp nearby," she said cheerfully. "Lands sakes, our electric bill is so high, we only run the lights at night. I have no idea how two old people can use so much electricity, but somehow we do!"

"I think I might have an explanation for that. Do you know anything about an extension cord plugged directly into your meter?"

The confusion on her face was answer enough. "An extension cord? Why would we have an extension cord out there? Gus doesn't do his woodwork anymore. Bursitis, you know. It ails him something terrible."

Brash sympathized with the elderly woman before asking, "Do you know your neighbor through the woods, Dickey Fowler?"

She tried to keep the disdain from her face, but traces of it slipped into her frown. "What has he done now? Every few weeks, the county law comes by, asking the very same thing. Usually wants to know if we know his whereabouts. As if we keep up with that boy!" she sniffed.

"I don't suppose you've seen him in the last day or so?"

"I can't remember the last time I saw him. It's been a good month or so, and that was only when we passed him in the car. We avoid the dirt road when we can, usually taking Thompson Road out this way. But what's this about an extension cord, Chief?"

"I suspect Fowler has been piggy-backing on your meter, using your electricity to run power to that shack he lives in."

"Lands sake, that can't be true!"

Brash gave a sad nod. "It sure looks that way. I'll call the electric company to come out and check, and to make certain this sort of thing won't happen again. I'm terribly sorry, ma'am, that he's been bilking you this way."

"That Dickey Fowler has always been a troublemaker, but I never dreamed he could do something like *this*! Gus and I can barely make ends meet, without him stealing our electricity!"

After a few more moments commiserating with the elderly woman, Brash said goodbye and retraced his path through the woods. He left the cords where they lay, but unplugged them at every coupling.

When and if Dickey Fowler returned to that dump, his fifty-inch television wouldn't do him much good without juice.

8

There were only a handful of houses scattered along that end of the county road, but none of the neighbors had seen Dickey Fowler recently. Most reported avoiding the surly young man whenever they could.

Brash visited all the man's known haunts, but no one claimed to have seen him in several days. Someone thought he had a new girlfriend; he was probably shacked up with her somewhere, living off her paycheck. She had some important job in Navasota, they thought. Or maybe it was in College Station. Whatever it was, Fowler bragged that it would make for a very nice Christmas.

With no other leads on Fowler's whereabouts, Brash returned to the police station. Just as he pulled into the old depot, he heard the call for a burglary in progress. Lights and sirens blaring, Brash wheeled out of the parking lot and sped that way.

The hysterical homeowner was on her front lawn when he reached the house.

"Mrs. Bashinski! Is there someone still in your house?" he asked, gun drawn as he leapt from the car.

"No," she sobbed into her shaking hands. "He ran away. That way!" She flung her arm in the direction from which he had just come.

"Are you certain?"

"Yes. No. Maybe he went that way." She pointed in the exact opposite way. "I don't know. Maybe there were two of them." She buried her face into her hands again.

"Ma'am, stay here. Do not come inside unless I tell you to do so."

Brash approached with care, working his way to the front door of the residence. He sidestepped a trio of wise men and a baby Jesus in his manger. The door was still ajar, the keys still dangling from the lock. According to dispatch, Mrs. Bashinski came home and surprised the man as he rifled through Christmas presents under the tree.

After a thorough sweep through the house, Brash put away his weapon and returned to the yard. Several neighbors had gathered on the lawn to console the distraught woman.

"I came home early from work," she told a neighbor. "I wasn't feeling well, and the principal told me to take the rest of the afternoon off. He would find an aide to cover my class."

"Ma'am, if you would, please come this way," Brash said, his voice firm but gentle. He took the fourth-grade teacher by the arm and gently tugged her away from her friends.

"What is going on here, Brash?" one man demanded. "Why are all these burglaries happening?"

"I say it's a gang, moving in here from the city!" another woman declared. "Hoodlums and drug addicts, thinking we're an easy mark!" A murmur of agreement rustled among her friends.

"When are you going to put a stop to this, Chief?" another man wanted to know. "Someone could have gotten hurt here today!"

Brash turned to the crowd, seeing a mixture of fear and anger upon their faces. "Did any of you see anything today? Did anyone get a look at the assailant?"

No one had seen a thing. The police sirens drew them from their homes.

"I need to question Mrs. B, so we can get to the bottom of this. Please, go back to your homes. I or one of my officers will be by later to see if you might have remembered something."

"We want answers, deCordova!" the first man blustered angrily.

"And so do I, Mr. Gale. That's why I need to talk with Mrs. B and give her my full attention. Please, go back to your own homes."

Grumbling, the crowd slowly dispersed.

"Mrs. B," Brash said, calling her the same thing her students did, "are you comfortable talking on your porch, or would you feel better talking in the squad car, or down at the station? We can't go inside yet, until we can dust for prints and see how the perpetrator entered."

"I—I want to stay. It won't take long for prints, will it?"

A second patrol car arrived on scene. "I hope not. Here's Officer Perry now."

Marilyn Bashinski couldn't tell him much. She came home almost two hours earlier than usual and surprised a burglar. After taking one step through the door, she spotted a man kneeling by the tree, tossing Christmas presents aside. He had a half-dozen small boxes already ripped open, their contents spilled on the floor. She screamed, he jumped, and both of them ran out the door. She called 9-1-1 from the front yard.

"He—He appeared to be looking for something," she said. "He only seemed interested in the smaller boxes."

"Had you ever seen the man before?"

"No. Maybe." She shook her head in frustration, cradling her cheeks. "Oh, I don't know. It all happened so fast. And he had a beard. A long, shaggy beard, like those men on TV."

Brash pulled out his phone and scrolled to the picture Bethani had taken. "Was this the man?"

"Possibly. But he wasn't wearing a uniform. He had on some sort of work shirt. Blue, I think. Maybe with an emblem, but I'm not sure. It all happened so fast," she repeated.

"I understand. And you're doing fine, Mrs. B, just fine. Let's go back to the Christmas presents. You say he seemed to be looking for a particular gift, something small. Do you have any idea what that could have been?"

"I don't know. Jewelry, maybe? Gift cards? I don't know!"

When his phone jingled with the ringtone for Maddy— *Pretty Woman*, by Roy Orbison—he took the call.

"Hi, sweetheart," she greeted. "How's your day going? Am I catching you at a bad time?"

"Actually, you are, but you might be able to help. Are you busy?"

"Nothing that can't wait."

"Could you come over to Mrs. Bashinski's house? Lemon Street in Naomi. Do you know the one?"

"The cute little blue craftsman on the corner, across from Weldon Gale?"

"Yes, that's the one. There's been another burglary, and I think she could use some company right about now." He looked at the trembling schoolteacher and offered an encouraging smile.

"That's terrible! I'm on my way."

As he tucked his phone away, Brash spoke in a calming voice to the homeowner. "A friend of mine, Madison Reynolds, is coming to sit with you while Officer Perry and I go through the house. Would you like to call your husband and have him come home to be with you?"

"I'll send him a text, but there's no need to disturb his classes, too. He'll be home shortly. That's one nice thing about both of us being teachers. We have the same schedule." She offered a weak smile. "And yes, I know Madison. My husband has her twins in Social Studies. Very bright students, both of them. And of course, Madison has done wonders for our town, bringing in that television show to redo the Big House."

He didn't point out that Madison had nothing to do with it. Granny Bert and Genny had cooked up that scheme, much to Maddy's chagrin. She had been reluctant to even accept the offer, until Granny Bert manipulated the carpenter into making a deal too sweet to turn down.

Brash continued questioning the schoolteacher until Madison arrived, at which time he joined his officer inside the house. He knew Maddy could not only comfort the distraught woman, but gently question her without it sounding like an interrogation. Particularly at times like this, Brash regretted not having a female officer on the force. If that grant came through and he could afford to hire a third officer, he planned to look at female entrants first.

By the time Syd Bashinski arrived home, Brash cleared the house for entry and Madison had the schoolteacher sipping on a cup of coffee.

"Thank you so much for staying with me, Madison dear," the woman said as she hugged her goodbye.

"Absolutely. You're sure you'll be okay now?"

"Syd is here now, and I'll call our daughter Betsey to come over. We'll be fine, dear. You tell Granny Bert I said hello, you hear?"

"I certainly will. Call me if you need to talk, or if you think of something that might be important." She winked and nodded covertly toward Brash. "I have that inside track to the department, after all."

Mrs. Bashinski had been the one to bring up Madison's relationship with the police chief, giving it her wholehearted approval. She laughed now, squeezing Madison's hands. "You keep that track open, my dear. You two make a darling couple."

Blushing despite herself, Madison thanked her and made her exit. On the way down the steps, she sent Brash a text.

Let's compare notes.

"Brash, you look exhausted," Madison admonished as she opened the door for the police chief. "Are you even sleeping at night?"

"Not much." He slipped his arms around her and simply held her close, savoring her nearness. Some people scoffed at the sentiment, but this woman was his soul mate. Simply being near her rejuvenated him and made him whole. The funny thing was, until he re-met her eleven months ago, he never knew a part of him was missing.

"You can't keep up like this, Brash."

"I don't intend to. I'm close, really close. I can feel it."

"Yes, well, I feel knots all in your shoulders." She ran her hands over the broad expanse, noting how tense he was. "Sit down. I'll give you a massage."

"Not yet. I just need to hold you for a few minutes," he said, burying his face into her silky brown hair.

"I'm worried about you, Brash," she whispered.

"I'm worried about *you*. I don't think it was a coincidence you were robbed this week."

She pulled away to stare up at him. With a reluctant groan, he dropped his arms from her waist and took a seat in a nearby chair. She followed right behind, peppering him with questions. "What are you talking about? How would I be targeted? And why?"

When she began kneading his taut muscles, he moved to allow her better access. He didn't answer right away. She had discovered a particularly sensitive knot. "Ah, right there."

"You're tight as a drum."

"Work it, doll," he drawled, but grunted when she hit another sore spot.

"I'll make you a deal. I'll work on your shoulders as long as you keep talking. Tell me why you think I was targeted."

"You know I've been working on this organized gambling ring for the better part of a year."

He couldn't see it, but she nodded her head. "I remember it was tied in to the cockfighting out at the old Muehler place." A shiver ran through her as she recalled the bloody, despicable sport.

"And I suspect it's connected to the ongoing drug problem we have here."

"Makes sense. Crooks go where the money goes."

"I've been making the rounds this week, putting a little pressure on some of the known associates, letting them know I have my eye on them."

"And you think this is their response."

"One of the things I've learned in law enforcement is to never assume that something is coincidental. Always look for a connection, no matter how small."

"What's the connection here? Who do you think stopped me the other night?"

"Dickey Fowler, Jr. A lowlife thug who lives a few miles out of Naomi in a shack that has no indoor plumbing, no electric. Of course, that didn't stop him from hooking up to his nearest neighbor and siphoning their electricity."

"You're kidding! How terrible."

"What I said. Ah, yeah, do that." She used her elbow to work out a stubborn knot of nerves and muscle. "You know, you should add masseuse to your—umph!—resume. You're good at this, even though you're killing me." When she let up, he hastily added, "No, don't stop. It hurts, but it helps. Ah, yeah, like that right there." Another grunted, "Umph."

"How did you know it was this Fowler person that stopped me?"

"I recognized his picture. That was smart of Bethani to think of taking it."

"You know teens. They document their entire lives on their smartphones. So, did you bring the guy in for questioning?"

"I went to his house, for lack of a better word. He wasn't there, but a crumbled game warden uniform was. Turns out, his uncle was a game warden who died on the job. His mother, Lois Fowler, was next of kin and inherited his last effects."

"So why would this Dickey Fowler person deliberately rob me? Is he tied up in the gambling ring?"

"I've heard his name mentioned in conjunction with it a time or two, but I understood he was just a participant, not an organizer. But get this. He is a distant relative to Bernie Havlicek, who *is* tied up in the ring, and who I *did* go to visit this week."

"Why does Bernie Havlicek's name come up in just about every crime that happens here?"

"Because the man is a weasel. He's crooked, but he's smart. He has his fingers in just about anything illegal you can think of, but he always manages to weasel his way out of being collared for the crime."

"Bend your head forward," she instructed, working her magic on his neck.

"On second thought, don't add massages to your list of services. I'm keeping this all to myself."

"You probably should see a professional. These knots in your muscles are ridiculous."

He grunted again before saying, "You have no idea how much you've already helped."

She worked for a moment in silence and then asked, "But how did this Fowler know I would be on the road that night? Do you think he's been following me?" At a new thought, she wailed, "Please don't tell me someone has bugged my house again!"

"I don't think they've bugged the house, but it's possible someone put a tracker on your car. I'll check it over before I leave."

"Which will be after dinner. I'm not letting you leave until you've had a good, hot meal. A little birdie tells me you haven't been eating right, either."

He pretended to growl. "I liked it better when you were intimidated by Vina, not best friends with her."

"To be honest, I'm still scared of her, just a little."

"You and me both," he muttered. He changed the subject with, "So tell me what you found out from Mrs. B."

"Not a lot more than you did. The burglar seemed to be after the smaller presents, Mrs. B startled him as much as he startled her, and he ran out the same door as she did, instead of going out a back way. I found it a bit strange."

"Which part?"

"All of it. For one thing, why would he risk getting so close to her? She could have tripped him, or hit him over the head, or something. It would have been smarter to run out the back door."

"Dickey Fowler fits the description she gave of the burglar, and Dickey Fowler doesn't exactly cook on all four burners. He comes from a long and disgusting line of inbreeding. Don't ask for details," he warned. "They'll turn your stomach, same way they did mine."

"So maybe that explains why he would look for jewelry under the tree, instead of in a jewelry box like most people. That was something else that didn't make sense."

"We don't know he was looking for jewelry," Brash pointed out. "It's a logical theory, but he could have been looking for something else."

"There was one thing, though. Mrs. B told me she did a good bit of her shopping this year at *Premium Jewels,* that new jewelry store that opened up in the mall." Brash's muscles tightened again under her hands, but he didn't interrupt her story. "Apparently they had one whopper of a Black Friday sale. Mrs. B bought diamond studs for most of the women on her list, a garnet bracelet for her friend, and a really nice gold watch for her husband. Even on sale, she said it was the most expensive thing she's ever bought him."

Madison could hear the frown in his voice. "She didn't tell me a watch was stolen."

"That's because she trick-wrapped it. You know, tiny box inside a small box, small box inside a medium box, medium box inside a great big box. Lots of Styrofoam peanuts to make a mess everywhere."

"So, you're wondering if the burglar somehow knew about the watch and was looking for it. Good possibility."

"Yes, but how? How would he know she bought the watch to begin with?"

Brash pulled away from her hands, thanking her for the much-needed massage. "There's several ways he could have known. He could have been in the store when she bought it. He could have overheard her telling a friend about it. The salesperson may have inadvertently let it slip. Could have been an inside job."

"You think Dickey Fowler works at *Premium Jewels?*"

"The only thing Dickey Fowler works at is getting into trouble. And even though he fits the description of the burglar, we don't know for certain it was him. Maybe it was, maybe it wasn't. Either way, the jewelry store isn't the only possibility for an inside job. Maybe the burglar works for the warranty company. Maybe Mrs. B. registered the watch online and the burglar or someone he knows hacked her account. Maybe he works at the bank and saw the debit card transaction. Maybe the burglar, especially if it was Dickey, got the information secondhand. There are literally dozens of possibilities."

Madison scrunched her face in playful distaste. "Here I thought I might be on to something, and you have to go and get all detective mode on me, bringing probability into it."

"Possibility, sweetheart, not probability," he told her. He tugged her forward so that she more or less stumbled into his lap. "And you were right, you might be on to something. It's worth checking out." He let his blue gaze wander down to her mouth. "And so are your lips," he murmured huskily. "What do you think the possibility is that I can get a kiss or two, or ten?"

Weaving her fingers through his dark-auburn hair, Madison thrilled at the sexy warmth of his voice. "We're not talking possibility," she corrected. "Not even probability. We're talking a sure thing. Pucker up, Chief deCordova."

A dozen kisses later, Maddy laid her head against his chest and listened to the steady pump of his heart. His arms formed a nice cocoon around her.

"How's the research coming with the Hutchins and the Carrs?" he asked.

"You were right. The Hutchins house is like the North Pole on crack."

"You do know you're starting to sound like Blake," he laughed. "And yes, they do go a bit overboard, don't they?"

"I have honestly never seen so many decorations in all my life. It makes me doubly appreciate my less-is-more concept around here. Granted, 'less' is all I could afford this year. Come to think of it, it's probably all I can afford until the twins are out of college."

"I think what you've done looks perfect."

"Thanks. As for the investigation, they've given me their guest lists and I've checked out about half the names. The guys who delivered the freezer have impeccable records of employment, the boys who worked on the lawn turned out to be ace students in school with excellent reputations, the Avon woman is Reverend Wallace's sister, the paper boy is ten, and most of the women who come to Bunco are connected to Vanessa through church. But I'm working on it, slowly but surely."

"And the Carrs? Anything the two cases have in common?"

"They are like polar opposites. Where Vanessa Hutchins is cheerful and upbeat, Mona Carr is sarcastic and rude. And she's a flat-out liar, Brash. They are cheating the insurance company, claiming all sorts of false purchases." She told him the discrepancies she found and why she suspected fraud.

"I'll give them a call," he promised, "and mention that lying to the adjusters is the same as committing theft against the insurance company. What about either of those cases, compared to the Bashinskis? Anything jump out at you as similar?"

"Mrs. Hutchins mentioned stealing a Black Friday deal from—oops, bad choice of words. Of '*out-shopping*' two of the junior high teachers on Black Friday. The B's are both teachers. Could that be anything?"

"I doubt it."

"I didn't think so, but it's about all I see so far, other than the whole Christmas gift angle." She lifted her head from his chest to look at him and ask, "Isn't it possible that the thefts are random? That it's just someone out to make an easy score, knowing people are Christmas shopping this time of year?"

"Of course it's possible. But it's my job to ignore coincidence and look for confirmation."

Madison couldn't help but tease him. "And by your job, you really mean the one you handed off to me."

"At a very reasonable hourly rate, I might add."

She accepted his light kiss before snuggling against him again. "As soon as I cross-reference and clear all the people who had access or interactions with the victims, I'll start cross-referencing the presents. See if they happened to shop in the same place, that sort of thing."

Brash smiled down at her proudly. "I knew I made a wise choice, hiring *In a Pinch* as a consultant. You sound like a professional investigator."

"Watching you, I'm learning from the best."

"Good thing neither one of us is prejudiced."

She returned his smile. "Yeah, isn't, though?"

9

Granny Bert fully supported the twins' plans for the Cookie Campaign, as Bethani dubbed it. She volunteered to buy the initial supplies, as long as they made enough cookies to stock her own jars. Granny Bert liked to bake ahead and freeze as much as possible, given the many events and parties she attended—and hosted—during the holiday season. This way, she said, they all came out winners.

For the next several days, the kitchen at the Big House looked more like a sugar war zone than it did the normally tidy retreat Madison had come to know and love. Because of the extra space in the newly remodeled kitchen, Granny Bert had agreed to do the baking there, rather than at her house. She also cited the disaster Blake created during their Mother's Day bake-a-thon.

When they went through the first round of supplies at an alarming rate, Genny stepped up and said *New Beginnings* would donate whatever else was needed. With her and Megan helping, the family whipped out dozens of delicious creations.

The aroma of freshly baked cookies wafted throughout the old mansion and lent a special sweetness to the holiday season. Who needed sugarplums, Blake quipped, when they had visions of cookies dancing in their heads, and, most importantly, in their tummies?

With the help of Jamil's father Demarco, Blake created the texting system for their Cookie Campaign. The girls made signs that explained the process. Text the number 266543— cookie, in numeric—while within fifty feet of the Big House and wait for a surprise response. It could be anything from a song, a special Christmas story or remembrance, or, if callers were lucky, the announcement that stated, 'Please meet us at the gate to accept your gift of Christmas cookies.' Calls from the same number were only granted cookies once, but they soon discovered that recipients came time and time again, simply to enjoy the lights and hear the random voice offerings.

Each night, a long line of cars made the corner on Second and Main to enjoy the new tradition.

One evening, dashing out to the curb with a bag of gingersnaps, Madison was surprised to see the driver behind the wheel of a shiny new Mercedes. The last person she expected to celebrate the holidays, particularly at her house, was Barry Redmond.

"Hello, Barry," she said, forcing out a congenial smile. "On behalf of my family, Merry Christmas! We hope you enjoy your cookies."

He batted the cookies away, knocking them to the ground. "I've reported you to the city council, you know," he snarled. "You're creating a traffic hazard! Just look at all these cars. There are vehicles backed up all the way to the railroad."

"I have the perfect solution for you, Barry," she said, keeping her voice even and pleasant. "Stay on your side of the tracks and don't venture into Juliet. Problem solved."

"You think you are some sort of princess, but you don't have royal blood. You're not related to Bertram Randolph in any way."

"And thank the Lord, or else I would be related to you."

If he heard her muttered statement, he chose to overlook it. He continued with his rant. "Yet you live in Juliet Randolph's house! It should have remained in the Randolph bloodline."

"Don't you ever get tired of this ridiculous vendetta of yours? Juliet Randolph didn't have children of her own, so she willed this house to my grandmother."

"Her cook's daughter!" he spat. "A servant!"

It was Madison's turn to ignore the interruption. "Granny Bert sold it to me. It was all perfectly legal, perfectly legit. If you're offering to buy the house from me, it's not for sale."

"I may take you to court and sue you for it, but I can promise you, I wouldn't pay you a red dime for this house."

"Good, because I prefer silver dimes." She stepped back from the car. "If you don't mind, Barry, you're holding up traffic and creating a hazard."

"Why you—you …!" Outraged, he could find no suitable term to condemn her with.

"Surely you have better things to do with your time than to harass me," Madison said. She flashed a fake smile and suggested, "Like looking for wife number five, perhaps?" She moved further away from the curb. "Bye now. Merry Christmas."

She turned her back to the glowering banker, feeling his hatred burn through her blouse. She had more important things to worry about than Barry Redmond.

For starters, she had to find time to re-buy all the gifts for the Angel Tree.

"You see what I mean?" Granny Bert beamed at her grand-daughter as they exited the hardware store. "*Now* do you see why it's so important to buy local?"

"Yes, Granny, they were very generous."

"Generous? They matched every dollar you spent, nickel for nickel! You went in for three bicycles and a skateboard. You came out with four bikes, two skateboards, and one of those new fan-dangled scooters. You wouldn't have gotten that deal at one of your fancy box stores, young lady. No ma'am, they wouldn't have donated a thing, unless you submitted it in writing to their board of overpaid executives, sometimes prior to the Ice Age. You couldn't walk in one of their stores and walk out the same day with a deal like this."

"No, but I could have shown a Groupon and gotten the same deal on the scooter."

"What in tarnation is a Groupon?"

"It's an online coupon that's good for—oh, never mind. You're right. Mr. Evans was very generous." It was easier to admit defeat than argue with her grandmother, especially when she was on her soapbox. "Who's next?"

"Jolene Kopetsky's resale shop, but maybe I'd better sit this one out."

Madison was immediately suspicious. "Granny Bert, what did you do?"

"Nothing."

"You said that too quickly and too innocently. Spill it." Madison got behind the wheel and slid her sunglasses into place. Even though it was the middle of December, the sun was bright and it was a balmy seventy-five degrees. The weatherman kept promising a cold front, but he had yet to deliver.

"I might have heard she was sniffing around where she doesn't belong."

"She was flirting with Sticker again, wasn't she? I heard about that display she put on at the Lion's Club Christmas party."

"Made a darn fool of herself, fawning all over the man, and with me sitting right there by his side!" her grandmother sniffed, fastening her seatbelt at her waist.

"So, what did you do?"

"Why do you think I did anything, girl?"

"Because I know you. And because you've been in every single store so far, giving them all the hard sell. Now you suddenly want to sit this one out. So, what gives?"

"I'm eighty-one years old, Madison Josephine. A body gets plumb tuckered out, hopping in and out of a hot vehicle all day long."

Unfazed by her grandmother's empathic claim, Madison shook her head. "You're trying too hard to convince me, Granny. We both know you have more energy than I do. Tell me the real reason you don't want to go inside Mrs. Kopetsky's store."

"Because she's a spiteful old woman who will take her personal grudge against me out on those poor, innocent, needy children."

"I'm already sold on the program, Granny. Just tell me what you did."

"Oh, all right! I may have put soap shavings in her egg salad to prove she's a mediocre cook, at best. Nothing's more embarrassing than taking home a full dish because no one will eat your cooking."

"Granny!" Madison cried in dismay.

"She had it coming. She knows Sticker Pierce is stepping out with me. She not only disrespected our friendship, she made a spectacle of herself and gave widows worldwide a black eye!"

Madison bit back a smile. "Flirting with your boyfriend and asking him to dance is not giving widows worldwide a black eye."

"You didn't see the dance, girl. She did the down and dirty with him, right there in the middle of the Lion's Club dance floor."

"I did hear it was rather... risqué," Madison admitted. She had heard a few other adjectives, as well, 'comical' being one of them.

"So, I think it's best I sit this one out."

Madison sighed. "You might have a point." She pulled up to the business and gave her grandmother a sharp look. "Can I depend on you to stay out of trouble? You won't egg her windows or anything like that, will you?"

"Not before you've gotten her donation, I won't."

"She might not donate anything. She might sell me the items at full price."

"Not if you play your cards right. Mention that I'm feeling poorly, after racing around town gathering donations from all the generous merchants. Play me up to be a saint."

"And you think that will encourage her to donate something to the Angel Tree?"

"I don't know, but it certainly can't hurt. Make her think twice about who's she up against."

"Granny Bert! This isn't about you, you know."

"Then do this. Throw in the clincher. Tell her I said that if we could get every single merchant in town to match our purchases, dollar for dollar, I promised to stay home all evening and wrap presents. Tell her she's the last one on the list, and if she doesn't participate, you lose the bet and have to wrap the gifts by yourself."

"Why should she care if I have to wrap them all myself?"

"Because tonight is the Knights of Columbus party, and she made Sticker promise to save her a dance. She'll donate half her store, just to make certain I stay home tonight and wrap."

"But Sticker is out of town, visiting his newest great-grandchild."

A broad smile broke across Bertha Cessna's wrinkled face. "Yeah, but she doesn't know that."

Madison was still laughing as she walked into *Good as New.*

As Jolene Kopetsky bustled to fulfill Madison's order and generously donated additional merchandise to equal *more* than twice the amount spent—it was such a good cause, after all, and what a shame Bertha would miss the party tonight—Madison visited with another shopper in the store.

"I heard what happened to you," the older woman said, "getting your car and all your presents stolen. What is this world coming to? And here in The Sisters, no less!"

"Oh, my car wasn't stolen," Madison corrected. "But it is true he stole all the gifts I had purchased for the Angel Tree."

"But pushing you down like that! That was completely cruel."

"He didn't push me. To be honest, I knew something wasn't right, but I didn't realize he was robbing me until he drove away, taking the presents with him." When she said it aloud, it sounded so foolish. How could she have not known? The lights had been so blinding, though, and she had been busy trying to get a covert call through to 9-1-1.

"I heard Molly Shubert's niece saw a man following you through the mall. After she heard what happened, she felt just terrible about not reporting it to security."

"Oh, well, I don't know about that," Madison frowned. So far, nothing else the woman heard was correct. She wasn't sure this was any different.

As Madison collected her wares and thanked the store-owner again for her generosity, Jolene beamed back at her. "It's the least we could do, especially since you're shopping local this go around. And you tell your grandmother I said bless her heart for helping you tonight. You tell her not to fret over her friend being left out. I'll invite him to sit at our table, just so he won't be lonesome."

Madison felt almost guilty as she returned the smile and said, "That's very thoughtful of you. I'll be sure and do just that. Bye, now. And thanks again."

"Oh, thank *you!*" the older woman gushed. She was already licking her lips in anticipation, fluffing her blue-gray bouffant as Madison walked out the door.

"Well?" Granny Bert demanded the minute Madison crawled into the car after stuffing her items inside.

"Worked like a charm. She donated more than I spent."

Granny Bert laughed triumphantly, rubbing her hands together in glee. "I can't wait to see her face tonight, when I walk into that KC hall!"

"But you promised to help me wrap gifts tonight."

"No, I said to *tell* her I promised I would. I never made such a claim. That's a horse of a completely different color."

"Granny, that's not fair! And that has nothing to do with a horse. It's got something to do with the back end of a similar but slightly different breed."

"Don't be calling your old granny names, girl. And don't be a sore loser. Let me off the hook tonight, and I'll tell you what I just saw."

Making no promises—two could play this horse game—Madison asked coolly, "What did you see?"

"I just saw Dickey Fowler hop on the weekly Greyhound. Looks like that boy is skipping town."

10

Madison couldn't reach Brash or either of his officers. Vina confirmed they were all out in the field, following a lead on the gambling ring.

Cutter was the next obvious choice. Not wasting time with needless questions, the chief of the volunteer fire department jumped in the fire engine and chased the bus down, catching up with it a few miles out of town. He eventually convinced the driver it was part of a new fire prevention break-check program. By the time he boarded the bus to offer his personal apology for the delay—and to sign autographs for female passengers who were fans of the home-makeover show—Dickey Fowler had exited through the emergency door and taken off for the woods.

"I'm sorry, Maddy," the firefighter apologized to his friend when they met up at *New Beginnings Café*. "He slipped out on me."

Madison was disappointed but sympathetic. "It's not your fault. And I hope you don't get in trouble for stopping the bus like that."

"Don't worry. I covered myself." He gave her an example of the charming smile that had gotten him aboard the bus in the first place.

Leaning over his shoulder as she poured another glass of sweet tea, his fiancé wasn't fooled for a moment. "Which is his way of saying the driver and half the passengers were female," Genny translated.

Cutter grazed her cheek with a kiss. "Don't be jealous, Genny darlin'. The bus driver was old enough to be my mother." With a glint in his blue eyes, he couldn't help but tease, "She was at least a year or two older than you."

"Watch it, buster, or I'll toss you out of here," she threatened in jest. "Didn't you see my new sign by the register? No shirt, no shoes, no *respect*, no service." She mussed his dark-blond hair with a devilish tease of her own. "Behave yourself, little boy."

For months, her best friend had fought her attraction to the man eight years her junior. Now that she had accepted the age difference—along with his marriage proposal—it had become a favorite joke between them.

Genny went on about her duties with other customers, leaving Madison and Cutter at the booth to talk.

"What can you tell me about Dickey Fowler?" she asked the fire chief.

"Not much, other than he's a thug."

"Brash thinks he's the one who not only robbed me, but Mrs. Bashinski, as well. So, it stands to reason he was in on the other crimes."

"I wouldn't put it past him. Stealing Christmas presents sounds about his style."

"At least he didn't ruin things for the Angel Tree program. The local merchants pitched in to replace everything that was stolen, and then some. We should have everything ready for Saturday's parade."

"I'll have the engine tanked up and ready to go. You have a Santa lined up, right?"

"Allen Wynn agreed to take over this year. He said he was eating plenty of Gennydoodle cookies to get him ready for his role."

Cutter laughed at the man's lame excuse for weight gain. "Blaming it on Genny, huh, and not his own lack of willpower?"

"Granny Bert said she's willing to overlook the fib because she's desperate. Something about Berle Shubert being sick this year, and not able to play his normal part."

"Berle Shubert has played Santa for as long as I've been involved in the parade. Being the local pharmacist, he knows most of the kids by name."

"That would come in handy," Madison agreed. "I can see where the kids would think he's the real Santa, knowing their names and all." She thought about the countless department store Santas she had taken the twins to see when they were young. Faced with an endless line of excited, noisy children, most of the costumed actors had been less than jolly. Not a one knew the children's names, not even the Santas at the country club. Given the exclusivity of Gray's favorite venue, the number of children visiting there with parents and grandparents was small; learning their names wouldn't have been so difficult.

Each day she lived here, Madison was reminded of the differences between small towns and cities. Madison was the first to admit that when she first returned, the small things had mattered most to her: no Starbucks in either of the towns, no mall, limited phone and internet providers, no home delivery from fast-food restaurants. Now, it was the big things that mattered: an invitation to have coffee in someone's home, stores with clerks who knew you not only by your name but by your family's history, a network of caring and helpful neighbors who shared information (particularly gossip) as quickly as any 4G carrier, and meals delivered by neighbors who knew you were sick or in need.

Madison smiled and added another important distinction between small towns and big cities: a Santa who knew the children by name.

"We won't let these Christmas Crimes ruin our holiday," Cutter insisted. "The parade will go on like always, and when it's over, we'll hand out bags for the Angel Tree."

"What about the rest of the children? Don't they notice?"

"All the kids get some small gift. The church ladies sew up little felt stockings and fill them with candy, coloring books, that sort of thing. They also make large Santa-style bags for the Angel Tree, so parents can claim the gifts came from the big guy himself. Those are handed out discreetly to parents while the kids are busy hearing Granny Bert, a.k.a. Mrs. Claus, read them a Christmas story."

"It sounds like a great tradition," Madison smiled. "And you are right. We won't let the Christmas Crimes, or Dickey Fowler, or anyone else ruin this for the children!"

With his prime Christmas Crimes suspect in the wind, Brash was more frustrated than ever. While Dickey Fowler was fleeing— first by bus, then by foot—Brash and his officers were chasing a dead-end lead on the gambling ring.

Another coincidence? Possibly, but he doubted it. An anonymous tip came in to the police station a half hour before the bus rolled into town. Brash and company rushed out, in hopes of finding the evidence they needed. That meant Dickey Fowler had ample time to leisurely board the outbound bus. Security cameras confirmed he hadn't even bothered with a disguise this time.

Maybe, Brash decided, he was too close to the case. Maybe he needed to put some distance between it and him. At least for the afternoon, he needed to get out of the office and away from work. Clear his head.

Deciding it was the perfect time to do his Christmas shopping, Brash took the afternoon off. Like Granny Bert, he preferred to shop local when possible. But for what he had in mind today, only a bigger town would do.

When Madison first mentioned *Premium Jewels,* he knew a moment of pure panic. Did she know he had visited the new jewelry store on numerous occasions, trying to decide on just the right ring? Did she know he had finally narrowed it down to two?

It took him another hour to do so, but after studying the two finalists and imagining them each on Maddy's hand, he finally made his decision. He chose the simple marquis diamond because, like his ladylove, it was long and elegant. Brash left the jewelry store with a much lighter wallet and a satisfied smile upon his face. He was even humming a Christmas carol while he finished the rest of his shopping.

It made for a late evening, but he marked off every item on his list. He treated himself to a celebratory treat on the way home.

While waiting in line for his food, he couldn't resist taking the ring out for one more peek. It truly was a stunning ring. He could hardly wait to place it on Maddy's finger...

"Sir? Here's your cheesy fries."

The woman's voice jolted him back to reality. Brash looked up and realized he was so lost in his fantasy, the woman at the take-out window had to repeat herself. For good measure, she shook the bag she dangled toward him.

"Oh. Sorry." Embarrassed to be caught daydreaming, Brash snapped the velvet ring box closed. He took the food bag with a sheepish smile and a hurried, "Thanks." Pausing only long enough to stow the ring away inside the glove compartment, he couldn't pull away from the window fast enough, particularly when he saw the woman's knowing sneer.

"Guess she's not a romantic," he muttered aloud. He popped a hot cheesy fry into his mouth as he pulled his truck onto the highway. As this trip was strictly personal, he had left the police cruiser at the station.

On the way home, he plotted the best way to give Madison the ring. Should he wrap it and put it under the tree? Slip it into her stocking? Go down on one knee and present it under a sprig of mistletoe?

That last thought made him rub his knee in silent protest. These old joints popped enough without aggravating them more. Maybe he should skip the 'on bended knee' idea.

He still hadn't come up with a plan of action by the time he crossed the River County line. He wanted something romantic. Something she would always remember.

Five miles out of Juliet, he rounded a curve and saw break lights ahead. One car sat sideways in the middle of the road, as another came to a stop behind it. Easing his truck off onto the side of the road, Brash grabbed his handheld radio and got out to offer help, calling in the plates as he approached.

He bypassed the second car and went around to the driver's side of the sedan dominating the two-lane highway. He made a quick assessment before rapping on the window.

Female driver, twenty-one years of age, brown hair. On her way home from work, if the uniform she wore was any indication. Stunned expression on her face, rigid posture. Shock, or something close to it.

"Ma'am?" he called through the glass. "Are you all right? Can I help you?"

With jerky movements, she turned toward him and nodded her head. She glanced nervously into the rear-view mirror, then at Brash. When she just stared at him, he motioned for her to roll down her window.

He didn't wait for it to go all the way down before asking in concern, "Miss? Are you okay?"

"Y—Yes, I'm fine," she stuttered. "A deer ran across the road." She looked into her mirror again, as if expecting it to return at any moment. "I swerved and... ended up like this."

Her foot was still on the brake. Brash stepped forward just enough to assure himself that her car wasn't damaged. "Looks like you managed to miss it," he confirmed.

"It all happened so fast."

When she darted another nervous glance into her rear-view mirror, Brash worried she exhibited signs of shock. "Will you be able to drive, ma'am, or shall I call someone to come get you?"

She looked momentarily panicked, as if giving personal information to a stranger frightened her.

"It's all right, miss. I'm an officer of the law."

"I—I'm fine," she repeated. She sat up straighter in her seat and vigorously shook her head, causing her hair to shake loose of its confines. Something about it struck Brash as odd. Perhaps it was the new strength in her voice as she insisted, "Seriously, I'm fine. I should get out of the road."

"If you're sure..."

"I am."

He barely had time to step away from the car before the young woman stomped her foot onto the gas and shot forward. The car wobbled as she struggled to contain it within the lane markings.

Brash scowled. Had the near-accident not taught her a thing? Speed may have been a factor in the ordeal to begin with. He considered going after her and issuing a citation, but the second car started forward, thwarting immediate progress back to his truck.

Deciding the young woman had suffered enough trauma for one night, Brash chose to give her a break. Besides, it was the holiday season. Christmas cheer, and all that.

He kept an eye out for wildlife as he made the short trek into town. Pulling up at home, he gathered all his packages from the seat and popped open the glove compartment.

A block of icy dread sank his heart right down to his toes.

The ring was gone.

11

If the perpetrators of the Christmas Crimes hoped to capture the police chief's attention, mission accomplished.

By stealing the engagement ring intended for Maddy, the criminals had vaulted their way into becoming his new number one priority. For now, even the gambling ring was pushed to the back burner.

The plate number for the girl in the road turned out to be fake, registered to a wrecked Chevy van that currently took up residence at *Bobby's Boneyard* in Riverton. The car he had seen in the middle of the road fit the description of hundreds of vehicles in the county. A light-colored basic sedan, completely forgettable.

Brash blamed himself for not being more vigilant that night, for not paying closer attention. He had been thinking about the ring, his head still somewhere up in the clouds as he approached the stalled vehicle. He should have asked to see her license, he chided himself. Gotten her name. At least paid attention to what kind of uniform she wore. He thought he remembered seeing pink, but it had been dark. With no vehicle damage and no personal injury, he hadn't taken the event seriously enough.

Brash saw two possible scenarios.

One, the near-accident happened as the girl described. While Brash was out of his truck helping the startled driver, someone in the second car had seen an opportunity and taken it. Searching his unlocked truck—a foolish mistake he realized now, but Brash was focused on helping a driver in need—they discovered the ring, pocketed the tiny treasure, and drove off with Brash none the wiser. He didn't even know what kind of vehicle it had been. Dark blue, perhaps, or black. Maybe a Ford product, judging from the brake lights. A crime of convenience.

Possible, but it didn't explain why the girl had fake plates to begin with.

Two, the near-accident had been staged. While Brash stopped to render aid, an accomplice hid nearby, waiting to slip into his truck. That would explain why the young woman kept looking into her rear-view mirror. There were plenty of trees and shrubs along that part of the highway where a person could lay in wait. He had even seen the plastic bag still tied to the bush where Madison had been robbed. Definitely a secluded stretch of roadway, perfect for an ambush.

There remained the question of whether he was the intended target or simply a target at random. How would someone know he would be traveling the road that particular night, with a valuable ring in his possession? For that scenario to work, it would have to be an inside job from the jewelry store. Again, a definite possibility, but he had made the purchase hours ago.

The other likelihood was that this was an experimental endeavor, targeting random travelers. Staging an accident or

flat tire—such as was the case with the man from Riverton—
the thieves had no idea of whom they might stop or what they
might find, but the odds were favorable they would find something of value. It was the Christmas season, and many people
from The Sisters traveled this highway after a day of shopping
in the city. Again, a crime of convenience.

But it galled Brash to think he made breaking the law any
more convenient than it already was.

Brash retraced his trip in the daylight, stopping along the
road to look for clues. By day, the highway was a busy thor-
oughfare. It made getting out of his police cruiser difficult,
if not downright dangerous. Brash thought he detected faint
footprints in the bushes along the road, but the soil was dry
and the wind had it scattered like a covey of quails.

One thing he didn't see were any skid marks. If, indeed, a
deer ran out in front of her, the young woman hadn't ended
up sideways because she locked up the brakes.

Back at the mall for the second day in a row, Brash asked
to speak with the manager at *Premium Jewels*. As he waited,
he observed the clerks moving about the sparkling glass cases. He recognized a few of the faces from previous visits, but
one woman was new. She looked vaguely familiar, however.
Perhaps he had seen her at a different store, or maybe even in
The Sisters. To his relief, he didn't see the clerk who sold him
the ring.

Probably having a day off at my expense, he grunted to himself. *Commission on a ring I've already lost.*

A voice spoke from behind him. "I'm Tobey Washington,
manager of the store. How may I assist you, sir?"

Brash turned and saw a large black man, dressed in a
neat navy suit and tie. Extending his hand, he introduced

himself. "Brash deCordova, Chief of Police in The Sisters and Special Investigator for River County. Can we speak in private?"

The manager's face split into a smile. "I know who you are."

Brash leaked a weary sigh. "The television show."

"No. Front line, Aggie defense." With a roll of his bulky shoulders, the man assumed his old football position. "It's me, Coach. Big T."

Recognition dawned in Brash's returning smile. "Big T Washington, of course! How's life treating you, man?" They exchanged another handshake, this one more exuberant and punctuated with an affectionate slap to the shoulder.

White teeth flashed in the manager's dark face. "I can't complain. Doing pretty good for myself these days. Got a pretty little wife, three kids, and a mortgage. Livin' the dream, Coach, livin' the dream."

"I'm glad to hear it, Big T. Do you ever hear from any of the guys on the team?"

They exchanged a few minutes of small talk and reminiscing before Tobey led the way to his back office. Brash was surprised to see his own framed face upon the wall. It was a photograph of him presenting a much-deserved award to the former football player.

"How can I help you, Coach? Name it, and it's yours."

"I need your help on something, Big T. We've tried to keep it out of the news, but we've had a rash of burglaries in The Sisters over the last few weeks."

To his surprise, Tobey nodded. "I've heard about that. One of our associates is originally from Naomi and was telling me about it," he explained. With a perplexed frown, he added, "But I'm not sure how I can help you. Other than you and Danielle, I don't know a soul who lives there."

"To be honest, I'm not sure how you can help, either. But some of the items stolen were purchased here in your store. I'm trying to see if I can establish some sort of connection."

"Wait a minute. You're not accusing one of our associates of something illegal, are you?"

"No, no, nothing like that," Brash assured him. "At least, not at this point. I'm simply following leads."

"You won't find any here," Tobey Washington said with confidence. "Given the nature of our merchandise, we do strenuous background checks on all our employees. If they have as much as a smudge on their record, we don't hire them."

"It might not be an employee. It could be a customer. Have you noticed any suspicious-looking people hanging around the store?"

The manager bristled. "You mean black men wearing hoodies?"

"No, I mean anyone, male or female, black, white, or polka dotted, hanging around for extended periods of time. Maybe they keep their heads down or angled away from the cameras. Maybe they keep their hands in their pockets. Do you recall anyone like that? Someone who looks nervous or out of place in a fine jewelry store?"

"You're describing a fourth of our customers. Ain't no harm in lookin', man. Everyone likes to look. Everyone likes to dream."

"Of course they do. But help me out here, Big T. You're a salesman. You know how to read a customer."

He pursed his lips in thought for a few moments. "Can't say I remember anyone in particular. We've been running some big sales, doing a lot of advertising. It brings in folks from all over. All walks of life, too. If I had a dime for everyone who's walked through those doors just to look, I could retire tomorrow."

Brash glanced at the oversized television screen hung from the ceiling. With one glance, the manager could view real-time footage of a half-dozen angles throughout the store. "You keep that footage on tape?" he asked.

"Of course. It backs up to the corporate server. After thirty days and at their discretion, they either save it or delete it."

"Any way I can get a copy of last night's footage?"

Not one to let personal connections get in the way of professional duties, the manager countered with, "Can you tell me why?"

Brash hesitated before divulging the full story. "The latest item stolen was purchased here yesterday afternoon. I'd like to see if I recognize any persons of interest in the background, or anyone casing the place."

"But we haven't been robbed, man."

"No. The robberies have taken place either en route or inside The Sisters. It could be that someone is targeting their marks and following them home."

"Give me a minute. I can copy the feed onto a flash drive." He rummaged around in his desk drawer until he came up with a suitable storage stick. "You only need yesterday?"

"How far can you go back?"

"Without requesting it from corporate, seven days."

"I'll take the whole week, then," Brash said.

"This will take a few minutes."

"While we wait, maybe I could see your employee files? At this point, all I need are names and addresses."

When Big T bristled again, Brash remembered the man faced temper issues. "Is this a formal request?"

Brash did the thing with his brows, his signature half-frown, half-arched eyebrow that effectively put players—and criminals—in their place. "No. A formal request would be much more invasive."

"I suppose I can get you those," Big T grumbled. "But anything more, and I have to run it by corporate."

Brash nodded. "Understood." Then he recanted with, "Just one other thing..."

"Coach—"

He cut off his protest. "I just need to know which of your employees is originally from Naomi."

He jabbed a thick finger toward the screen. "Danielle Applegate. That's her at the necklace counter, showing that guy the opal filigree."

It came as no surprise that it was the woman he thought he recognized. He still couldn't place her, but he had probably seen her around town.

"Do you mind if I speak with her?"

Tobey hesitated before nodding. "I've always respected you, Coach. You treated us all fairly and you always believed in me. I'm giving you a lot of leeway now, because of that respect. If she is free and no customers are around to overhear, you may speak with her briefly. Anything more can't be on my dime."

"I understand that, Tobey, and I fully respect your position." Another glance at the monitor showed the would-be customer shaking his head in regret and moving away. "Ah, it looks like she's free now," Brash noted. "I'll have a word with her while you're finishing that flash drive."

Speaking with the officer made the sales associate nervous, but she slowly warmed to his questions.

Yes, she grew up in Naomi. Her aunt told her about the terrible rash of burglaries. No, she had no idea some of their merchandise had been among the items stolen, but it wasn't surprising, given the great promotions they offered. No, she hadn't seen any overly suspicious-looking people hanging around the store. A few nervous-looking young couples, perhaps, as they gazed at the engagement rings. One blond woman who stalked a particular ring, checking in daily to see if her boyfriend had purchased it yet. Nothing uncommon for a jewelry store, she laughed. Before this job, she worked at *Zale's*, so she was familiar with the patterns. She had seen nothing out of the ordinary.

With a clearing of his throat, Tobey Washington approached from behind and signaled the interview was over. "This should be everything you asked for."

Brash pocketed the flash drive with a smile. "Thank you, Big T. I really appreciate your help."

"No problem, Coach. I hope you find the answers you're looking for."

"I hope so, too." Brash cast a baleful glance at the ring counter, where another solitaire filled the empty space he had created just the day before. His voice turned mournful. "More than you can imagine."

12

Madison tucked the present under the tree amid the other colorful packages. This paper, the brown craft with camo wildlife silhouettes, was for Brash. Finding just the right gift for the special man in her life was difficult, but she thought she had finally pegged it.

With everyone else in bed, she took a few moments to soak in the silence. Even in a house this big, it was hard to find time to herself. She turned off the overhead lights and curled up in a chair, enjoying the lights from the tree.

This was their family tree, the one strewn with popcorn garland and a mishmash of favorite ornaments. The formal tree was in the ladies' parlor near the foot of the stairs, visible from the street through the front windows of the old mansion. That tree was decked out in shiny silver and gold. Simple and elegant.

But this tree was better. It had no theme, no rhyme or reason. The paper handprint cutouts, now impossibly small, were from the twins' earliest years. Scattered among the branches were personalized ornaments marking their obsessions at the moment: Barbie dolls, race cars, Power Rangers, Furbies, Beanie Babies, Buzz Lightyear. As the twins got older, the ornaments became more refined. Cell phones, a blinged-out megaphone, the mini football jersey with Blake's number on it. It was like a time capsule, hanging from the limbs of her Christmas tree.

There were tiny smiling faces in festive frames. Some were hers, some were Gray's. There were ornaments from her parents, sent from whatever faraway land they inhabited at the time. Souvenir ornaments picked up while on vacation. From where she sat curled beneath an afghan, Madison spotted a bauble from Disneyland, another from Colorado, the maple leaf from Vermont, the sand dollar from Galveston. The hot-air balloon blown from glass, depicting the day Gray proposed to her. Once upon a time, it was her favorite ornament of all, and each year, she and Gray took turns re-telling the story as they chose its place of honor upon the tree. This year, she had hesitated as she took it from its tissue. The memories surrounding it were now bittersweet. But Bethani had been watching her as she unwrapped it, and she had seen the sadness in her daughter's eyes. With a breath of courage, she had chosen a discreet and out-of-the-way limb for its temporary home. The gesture gained a watery smile from Bethani and a prick to her own heart.

More than a time capsule, Madison decided, this was her life, displayed among a thousand twinkling lights.

Her eyelids grew heavy and she began to nod off. Just before the old grandfather clock struck midnight, the doorbell rang. Madison jerked to attention, wondering who could be coming to call at such an hour.

Her first thought was of Bethani and Blake. Had there been an accident? But no, they were both in their rooms; if not asleep for the night, at least safe and secure. Genny, too, was tucked away in her corner suite.

Brash? He would have texted before coming over.

Worrying that something had happened to Granny Bert, Madison hurried to the door. She peered out the tiny peephole and let out a squeal. She couldn't open the massive door quickly enough.

"Mom? Dad? What are you doing here?" she cried.

"Merry Christmas, baby girl!" Charlie Cessna boomed as he wrapped his arms around her.

"Surprise!" her mother chirped, worming her way into the embrace.

They were all talking at once, a mingle of laughter and exclamations and tears.

"I can't believe you two are here! You never said a word!"

"Oh, baby girl, it's been too long! You look great."

"I love what you've done with your hair. Ooh, come here, you, and give your momma another kiss!"

A bleary-eyed Blake appeared on the second-floor landing. "Mom? What's going on?"

"Blake Reynolds, is that you?" Charlie boomed. "Get down here, boy, and give your grandparents a proper welcome!" It was so like her father to show up at midnight, unannounced, and expect a party.

With a whoop, Blake bounded down the stairs. Within minutes, Genny stumbled from her room, blond hair mussed and perky pajamas slightly off-kilter. She had a weakness for cute nightclothes, and they had been one of the first things she replaced after the fire. This was one of her holiday editions, which touted something about a naughty but nice elf who bore an odd resemblance to Marilyn Monroe.

At least five minutes later, Bethani joined the melee from her third-floor reign. "What is all the noise down here?" she grumbled. Then she caught sight of the grandmother she hadn't seen in three years, other than on Skype. "Happy? Is that you? Grandpa Charlie? You're supposed to be in Africa!"

"Surprise, Bethi-boo! Christmas came early this year. Now come down here and join the party!"

The party lasted until almost dawn. Genny pulled together middle-of-the-night omelets and pan toast, Bethani served Chunky-Charlie cookies (made earlier in the day for their Cookie Campaign) and Charlie kept them all entertained with tales of their missionary adventures.

While the twins and her mother hung on his every word, Madison studied her father. The years had been kind to Charlie Cessna. At first glance, he didn't look a year over fifty. His hair was still streaked with natural-blond highlights, with no gray in sight. He wore it long, pulled back and secured by a leather string braided with beads. Always in excellent physical condition, he may have put on a few pounds as he neared sixty, but he still struck a handsome pose. She noticed a few more lines fanning out from his laughing blue eyes, a few new age spots on his work-roughened hands. Madison knew that most people didn't classify his past careers as 'work.' Being in a rock band, driving race cars, and working as a stunt man sounded more like play to most people, but when Charlie Cessna did something, he gave it his all. Those callouses came from being the best at whatever he did, and doing it twice as hard as the next person. The only thing he never quite mastered was being a father.

No longer feeling any malice toward her parents for abandoning her, Madison smiled as her father told one outrageous tale after another. She knew to take anything her father said with a grain of salt. He told a story about facing down an angry mob of fifty natives in the jungles of Africa. She guessed the truth to be a dozen disgruntled locals, somewhere outdoors. Still, the tale was entertaining and had his audience sitting on the edge of their seats. Even her mother waited on bated breath to hear the outcome of the story.

Allie Cessna, known to her grandchildren as Happy, had aged a bit more than her husband. She was still a beautiful woman, trim of the waist and full of the buxom, but the harsh elements were taking their toll upon her skin. Too much time in the sun had turned her wrinkled and brown, but it didn't diminish her looks. Her eyes still twinkled with a smile and her words still came out on hushed breath, giving her a little-girl charm in an antique body. With her long, flowing gray hair and her gypsy-style clothes, she looked more like a flower child than a grandmother.

Her parents had married young and had their one and only child long before either were mature enough to handle parenthood. If she were being honest, Madison doubted her parents would ever be mature enough for that particular challenge. They were both free spirits that could not be tamed. She hadn't understood at the time, but leaving her with Granny Bert had been the best thing they could have done for her.

"What about Granny Bert?" she belatedly thought to ask. "Does she know you're home?"

"We went by there first. She shooed us out after a while, saying she had a big day tomorrow."

"Yes, the Christmas parade. In fact, if we don't go to bed now, there's really no sense." Already the first rays of light feathered the dark sky with pale color.

"Guess we have kept you up all night," Charlie said, a rare sheepish smile upon his face.

Madison hugged her father. "That's okay, Dad. Having you and Mom home for Christmas is worth the sacrifice."

All too soon, her alarm clock blared its wakeup call. Madison rolled over with a groan and hit snooze. Five minutes later, she dragged herself out of bed and into the day.

The Annual Sisters Christmas Parade alternated its route each year, so that both towns took turns hosting the event. This year, the lineup started in Naomi and wound around to its conclusion in Juliet. Two horse-drawn covered wagons, the horn section of the high school marching band, the Cowboy Church's mounted choir, a Girl Scout troop, a spattering of festively adorned golf carts and ATVs, three of Jimbo Hadley's goats fitted with reindeer horns upon their heads, and a half-dozen or so decorated trucks, some hitched with decked-out flatbed trailers, preceded Santa's arrival on the firetruck. At the end of the route, he and Mrs. Claus entertained young-sters at the 'North Pole.'

While Santa heard Christmas wishes and Mrs. Claus read stories and handed out treats, Madison helped in the background. She discreetly helped parents sign in to collect their Santa Sacks, which were filled with toys and much-needed necessities. According to those who helped with the event each year, this year's list of families in need was longer than ever.

It warmed Madison's heart, knowing she played at least a small part in making so many Christmas dreams come true. Making it even more fun, the event was almost like a family reunion. Having instilled a sense of community and generosity in her children and grandchildren, many of the volunteers were Granny Bert's own family. Pleased to be a part of that legacy, Madison was determined to make this another yearly tradition.

As the stack of Santa Sacks dwindled, Madison spotted Brash weaving his way toward her. Instead of his usual sexy smile, his lips wore a frown. He stopped before he reached the small crowd, hanging back to remain unnoticed.

"Uhm, can you take over for me?" Madison asked her cousin Hallie.

"Sure thing. In fact, we're almost done here. Go home and enjoy having Uncle Charlie and Aunt Allie home."

Another glance at Brash said he wasn't bearing good news. "Okay, thanks, Hallie. Today was fun." She hugged her cousin and slipped away to meet her somber-faced boyfriend.

She squinted up at him in dread. "Why do I think you didn't just drop by to see how things are going?"

He kept his voice low as he offered her a tight smile. "Because you know me too well. And you're right." With a heavy sigh, he said, "There's been another robbery."

"Oh no! What this time?"

"Allen and Mitzi Wynn. Mitzi just got home and found someone had broken in and stolen half their gifts."

"B—But—Allen's playing Santa Claus!" Madison sputtered in outrage.

"I know. Pretty low, huh? The guy dedicates his time to a community function and someone repays him like this." His voice was rife with disgust.

"This isn't like our towns, Brash. This is crazy."

"And I intend to put a stop to it, once and for all. I'm headed out there now. Can you get free?"

"Already done. Hallie's taking over for me."

"Then let's go talk to Mitzi." He took her elbow and ushered her toward his waiting patrol car.

"Does Allen know yet?"

"No, Mitzi said there was no need to ruin the day for everyone. He'll be done playing Santa in a half hour."

At the Wynn home on the outskirts of town, Mitzi Wynn paced the living room. She broke stride long enough to open the door and usher Brash and Madison inside.

"I hope you don't mind me bringing Madison along," the police chief said. "I've called her in as a private consultant to help with our investigation."

Mitzi answered by giving the other woman a grateful hug and a trembling smile. "Of course not! Allen and I were so pleased with the work you did for us last year, getting to the bottom of that boundary dispute with Hank Adams." Her smile faded as she added, "Even if things did get a little hairy for a while there. Again, Maddy, I'm so sorry. We never dreamed you would be in danger."

As always when the case was mentioned, Brash felt a rumble of unease in his gut. That was the time the drug boss had gotten away. For a moment, he wondered if last spring's drug bust and this recent break-in were related. But how?

"Don't be silly," Madison assured her. "You had no idea there was a drug lab on your neighbor's property. Even poor Hank had no idea. But please, tell us more about to-day's break-in."

Reminded of the here and now, Mitzi threw her hands into the air. "I can't believe someone would do this! They had to have known we would be gone this morning."

Madison nodded in agreement. "Half the town goes to the parade, but particularly the man who plays Santa Claus."

"That's the thing. Not many people knew Allen was filling in for Berle Shubert this year." She turned to pace again in frustration.

From the corner of her eye, Madison saw Brash jot down the information in his notebook. "Do you know what was taken?" she asked.

"We bought Bradley a Play Station and Connor a new basketball goal." She paused to offer a nervous laugh. "You should have seen me getting that thing in my car! By the time I crammed in the rest of the gifts, it looked like I was moving! The woman at the drive-through laughed at me for having to drive with the window cracked. It was the only way to fit the corner edge of that thing in there." She rubbed her forehead, aware that she was rambling. "It was the display model and already put together," she explained. "The last one in stock. Those were the boy's big gifts, and now they're gone!" She ended on a wail.

"Were they already wrapped?" Brash asked.

"No. We had them hidden in the storage shed out back."

A frown furrowed the policeman's forehead. This was a different tactic for the thieves, searching outbuildings. He noted the new MO before asking his next question. "Was it common knowledge you kept gifts in the outbuilding?"

Despite the situation, Mitzi found a playful smile to brandish his way. "We have two teenage sons. We hid gifts in the one place they would never think to look—behind the lawn mower and the chain saw."

"Were those taken?"

She shook her head. "Only the gifts."

"Was anything else stolen, besides the PlayStation and the basketball goal?"

This time, she nodded. "All the gifts we had in the shed, none of them wrapped. There was a large framed print for my mom, a Weed Eater for my dad, a little trike-thing for our niece." She touched her forehead again, thought for a moment, and named off one or two more items.

"And you noticed the break-in when you first got home?"

"Yes. I left the celebration early, so I could wrap gifts. I declare, Allen Wynn is as bad as a child when it comes to snooping around for his Christmas presents! I bought him a really nice watch this year, so I hid it somewhere he would never suspect... out in the shed, where we're hiding the boys' gifts. I went out to get it so I could wrap without him here, and that's when I discovered someone had broken in."

Madison sent Brash a sharp glance. Marilyn Bashinski had purchased a watch for her husband. Coincidence? Or connection?

His tone remained calm and steady, but Madison recognized the glint in his dark eyes. "Was the watch taken?" Brash asked.

"No. I had it well hidden, tucked inside my gardening glove, and the glove inside my gardening box. They only took the obvious things."

"Can you tell if any of your wrapped gifts are missing from under the tree?"

Mitzi stopped her pacing and practically fell onto the couch. She looked despondently at the tree and shook her head. "I don't think so. As you can see, I haven't done much wrapping yet."

"So nothing was taken from inside the house?"

"It doesn't appear they came inside. Officer Perry is outside now, looking for signs they tried to get in." She wrung her hands in distress. "Who is doing this, Brash? Things like this just don't happen here! We've always been such a safe community."

Weariness showed in Brash's face. Frustration and exhaustion weighed down his sigh. "I completely agree. But no community, no matter how small or how closely knit, is immune to crime. People move in, people travel through, and they bring their thieving ways with them. But I can assure you, Mitzi, we're working on this, and I am determined to find the culprits."

Madison knew Brash viewed the crime wave as a personal assault on his peacekeeping skills. She knew it was more than an issue of pride. This hit on a more vulnerable level, making him question his own abilities as a lawman and defender of the people. And when he hurt, she hurt.

None of those insecurities showed on his handsome face as he set his pen to paper. "So, let's go over this, one step at a time. Tell me everything."

Mitzi tossed her hands into the air once again. "What more is there to tell? While Allen was playing Santa Claus, someone else was playing the Grinch!"

13

Once Allen returned from his Santa duties, Brash and Madison talked with the couple at length. Afterward, Madison went home and shut herself inside her office for the evening. With the Angel Tree and parade checked off her to-do list, she could devote her attention to the Christmas Crimes. The silly term had stuck, and she now found herself referring to the case as such.

Filling in for her, her parents took charge of the Cookie Campaign for the busy Saturday night. Charlie was in his prime, visiting with old friends and chatting with every person who drove up. Happy strummed Christmas carols on her ukulele and sang in her whispery soft voice. A few friends from school joined Bethani, Blake, and Megan in handing out bags of cookies and Christmas cheer.

Madison was surprised to see Miley Redmond among the teens gathered on her lawn. Not only was she Barry's daughter, but she had long been a thorn in Bethani and Megan's adolescent sides. Madison had encouraged the teens to be more understanding of the other girl's plight. Perhaps, she told them, Miley's attitude was the result of an unhappy home life. Her mother was in and out of drug rehab and the teen lived with her father, a busy banker who had recently divorced his fourth wife and who spent paltry little time with his only child. After the events of the summer that emphasized how little Miley's parents appreciated her, Madison thought she detected a softening in her daughter's attitude toward the less fortunate girl. Miley had money, but that was a pale substitute for friends and people who genuinely cared.

With a pleased smile that Bethani and Megan were at least trying to be more compassionate, Madison turned away from the window. The festive atmosphere out on the lawn was a bit distracting, but she was determined to work on her case. Brash depended on her.

Taking a cue from the police chief, she pulled out her own whiteboard and her lists, and studied the similarities. There were scant few connections.

The victims had little in common. The Bashinskis were both teachers. Vanessa Hutchins worked at the pharmacy, Larry was an accountant. Reggie Carr worked as a car mechanic, and Mona didn't work at all, at least not outside the home. Mitzi was also a teacher, and Allen was a businessman. Reluctantly including herself in the count, she noted that she was a single mother who owned a (very) small business, Bethani a high school student. The other motorist robbed, Ted Berlin from Riverton, was a cattle buyer for a packinghouse. Only two of the couples attended the same church, and all ran in different social circles. She and the Wynns had the strongest connection and it was tenuous, as best.

The only other connection she found was weak, and it still didn't link all six cases together. Victims from two of the burglaries were teachers. That in itself seemed suspect, until she considered the fact that The Sisters Independent School District was the largest employer in the towns. A fourth victim had a shopping altercation with two other teachers within the district, and Bethani attended The Sisters High. She even had Mr. B as a teacher. Yet the whole school tie-in seemed irrelevant. For the life of her, Madison couldn't see how the school could be the common denominator.

Still, she underlined it as a possible connection.

After chasing down the names of Bunco players and recent visitors to all the homes, she found little of promise. One of the players was a teacher, another was Allen Wynn's sister-in-law. The Avon representative dropped a delivery off to Mitzi but left it on the front porch. Three of the victims had package deliveries from the same carrier, but further investigation showed only two of those had the same deliveryman. There was the faintest of connections with the cuckoo clock. Like Ted Berlin, the clocksmith lived in Riverton. After coming to Juliet to change out Vanessa's cuckoo, the older man dropped by to visit his distant relative, Syd Bashinski. The man, however, was over seventy and walked with a slow and painful gait. He came with a stellar reputation and no ties to anything remotely unlawful, making him an unlikely person of interest.

With so few people on her POI list, Madison concentrated on the presents stolen. Perhaps that would yield better clues.

It was difficult to know which of Mona Carr's reported losses were bogus, and which were real. Madison worked off the assumption that anything priced over fifty dollars was suspect. As she whittled down the lists, she found a few similarities that seemed worth pursuing.

Vanessa and Mona both made purchases at *Victoria's Secret*.

Ted Berlin, Mitzi, and Mona had purchased sporting equipment, just as she had.

Vanessa, Mrs. B, and Mona, if believed, shopped at *Premium Jewels*. Mitzi had also shopped there, but her jewelry purchases were still safely nestled beneath her tree or, in the case of the watch, hidden inside her garden glove.

All the victims had purchased some sort of small electronics and/or a game device.

All had shopped in the Bryan/College Station area. Again, not surprising, given the college town offered the largest selection of stores—not to mention the only shopping mall—in the area.

The robberies had even been conducted in different manners. Two homes, one vehicle, and one outbuilding were burglarized by forced entry. Two vehicles were robbed on the same road; one while the motorist was outside the vehicle, one while the driver (much to her dismay) was still inside. Three deeds by daylight, three by night.

Madison dutifully underlined all the common factors, noted their rate of occurrence, and studied the final list, pathetic though it was.

Twirling an invisible mustache, she mimicked Sherlock Holmes playing *Clue*. "It was the teacher, using a diamond-studded game controller, in College Station."

She dropped the playful attitude and blew out a defeated breath. "Who am I kidding? It could be anyone, using any method of entry. But one thing is for certain. It happened right here in The Sisters. And with Christmas just one week away, time is running out."

"The twins and I are going shopping," Happy announced the next afternoon. "Would you like to come with us?"

It was on the tip of Madison's tongue to refuse. She had a long list of things to do. Yet how often did she get the opportunity to go shopping with her mother? It would be three generations, out for a day of fun.

"Sounds fun," she decided.

"Great. Blake's already chosen where we're eating for dinner. Ready in five minutes?"

"Five minutes? But—" She bit her tongue and nodded. "Sure, Mom. Five minutes is fine. Let me get my purse."

Not for the first time, Madison secretly wondered if she were adopted. She had inherited none of her parents' spontaneity. While they acted on their impulses, Madison gave careful thought to her course of action. Going shopping meant making lists, gathering her meager stash of cash and coupons, changing into comfortable shoes.

Yet here she was, still dressed in her church clothes and the most uncomfortable pair of shoes she owned, headed to the mall, with no list in sight. Sure, she had her little Christmas notebook in her purse, the master list with shopping ideas and little check marks above the items already purchased. But she hadn't decided which stores to visit or plotted her shopping strategy. She hadn't even checked the weekly circulars to see which store offered the best deal. She said as much, as they neared their destination.

"It's called store apps, Mom," Bethani chided with a roll of her eyes. "Sign up for email blasts and text alerts, and you'll get all the latest sales on your phone. Here, hand me your phone and I'll put some in for you."

"To all *your* favorite stores, I'm sure."

The teen smiled sweetly. "The more money I save you, the more you can buy for me."

Madison tossed her own mother an exaggerated look, but she was smiling. "See what a thoughtful daughter I have? Always thinking of others."

"She has a point, Maddy. Today's world is online."

"Says the woman who lives in the jungles of Africa."

"It may not be quite as primitive as your father makes it out to be," Happy confided. "We do have a few luxuries in the village where we live."

"Speaking of my father… Dad seems to be enjoying himself now that he's home. I thought he was going to stay outside all night visiting!"

"He might have, for all I know. I finally gave up and went on up to bed," her mother sighed. "I suppose he's making up for lost time. We were in quarantine for what seemed like forever, you know, when we first left Africa. He's glad to be back among people again, particularly ones he hasn't seen in so long."

"He's always been in his prime when surrounded with people. Blake takes after him, I'm afraid. He's in the drama club at school and quite the performer, just like Dad."

"I can hear you, you know," her son said from behind the wheel. Madison had allowed him to drive on the way into town, promising the return honors to his sister. Having only recently turned sixteen, their driving skills were still new and evolving.

"Good. Then you'll hear me say slow down. Again."

"There's such a thing as impeding traffic, you know. I could get a ticket for going too slow."

"Not at this speed, you won't. Besides, we're almost to the exit for the mall."

Once inside the crowded stores, Madison wasn't sure how much shopping they were actually accomplishing. With four of them browsing together, their interests were pulled in different directions and different stores. Blake wanted to stop at every snack kiosk they came to. Bethani was drawn to every clothing store. Shopping for one another was impossible.

"Ooh, look, my phone just binged," the teen said, flashing her screen toward her mother. "*TossUp* is having a sale. Up to sixty percent off! And look at that top, isn't it the cutest?" She pointed to the outfit in the window.

"How did your phone know we were in front of the store?" Madison frowned.

"Again, it's called store apps, Mom."

"I think it's called Big Brother," she muttered.

She looked confused. "The television show?"

"No, the book. The all-seeing eye."

"You know… the internet!" Happy chirped. "And you're right. That top is the cutest! Come on, Bethi-boo, let's go check it out." Hooking her arm with her granddaughter's, the two sailed into the store before Madison could further protest.

After an hour of chaos, Madison finally gave in and allowed the twins to go off on their own, telling them to check back with her in an hour.

"I'll text you," Bethani promised.

"Fine. Have you seen Happy? I swear, she's worse than you kids, wandering off on her own."

"I saw her over by the shoes, talking to some guy," Blake offered. He used the bottom of his yogurt cone to indicate the direction.

"What guy? A sales clerk?"

"I don't think so. See you later. Beth and I have shopping to do!"

"Great," Madison muttered beneath her breath. "My gift will be a rubber ring from the arcade. Because if I know my son, that's exactly where he's headed. Now to find my mother…"

She wandered through the department store until she spotted her mother's long hair and distinctive flowing skirt. Sure enough, she was engaged in a lively conversation with a large man that Madison didn't recognize.

The closer she got to the man, the more surprised she was. He had rough features, exacerbated by the silvery scar slashed across his left cheek. His head was shaved clean and when he turned, Madison saw a crude tattoo at the back of his neck. Something about it screamed *prison*. Alarmed, she picked up her pace and hurried toward her mother.

She thought the man might be panhandling, taking her mother for an easy mark. He had bulging biceps beneath his too-short shirtsleeves. Tattoos ran the length of his muscled arm, some more professionally inked than others. To her surprise, her mother laughed at something the man said.

"Mom? I wondered where you had gotten off to."

"Oh, hi, Maddy. I just ran into an old friend and was catching up."

Friend? More likely someone from her outreach program, Madison thought.

"Tom, I don't believe you've ever met our daughter. Maddy, this is Tom Haskell, an old friend from back when your father was a croupier. Tom, Maddy."

"Why, Maddy, you are just as pretty in person as you were on TV," the behemoth of a man said.

Something about his smile made her distinctly uncomfortable. It wasn't the chipped and broken teeth, evidence of having had one fight too many. It wasn't the way his bottom lip rippled from the effort, poorly healed from being busted so often. No, the look in his eyes made Madison uncomfortable.

Look? she questioned. It was more of a leer. Like he knew something about her, something secretive.

She knew her smile was stiff when she said, "thank you" with little sincerity. "Mom? Are you done shopping?"

"Well, no, Maddy, I've been visiting." Her mother was clearly aggravated at her rude behavior, subtle though it was. "Tom and I have both been away for years and were catching up."

Madison tried, for her mother's sake. "Oh? And where are you from, Mr. Haskell?"

"Like your parents, I'm a traveling man," he said evasively. "I've just recently moved back to the Navasota area."

"I told Tom he really must come for supper one night," Happy prattled on. "Your father would get a kick out of seeing him again, after all these years!"

"I'm sure he would," Madison agreed. She touched her mother's arm. "I don't mean to rush you, but our day is slipping away. We have dinner reservations in an hour."

"Reservations? What are you talking about?"

"Blake made them," she said hastily, knowing her mother would not object to anything either of the twins might do.

An indulgent smile touched her mother's face. "Ah, I'm sorry, Tom, but my grandson is at that age. A bottomless pit that must be fed."

"I understand, Allie. No need to apologize. Don't forget to tell Charlie I said 'hey.'"

"Of course not! And I'm serious. Come over for supper some night, we'd love to have you. Wouldn't we, dear?" She turned to her daughter for confirmation.

Maddy's smile was tight, but she managed. "We'll set something up after the holidays. Do you have his number?"

"I gave him yours," Happy said, oblivious to the evil eye she earned from her daughter.

"It was very nice to meet you in person, Maddy," Tom Haskell said. "I feel like I already know you." There seemed to be a touch of laughter in his voice, but she could have imagined it. She reluctantly took the beefy hand he offered.

"You have a Merry Christmas, Mr. Haskell."

All but shooing her mother forward, Madison put as much distance between them and the man as possible.

"Madison Josephine, what was all that about? You were absolutely rude to that man! What has gotten into you?"

She ignored the questions and asked one of her own. "How do you know that man, Mother?"

"I told you, we knew him back in the day."

"The man is obviously a criminal, Mother."

"A criminal? What are you talking about?"

"Didn't you see those tattoos? The ones that looked more like ink blobs? That's because they are. Those were prison tats."

"One, you don't know that for certain. And two, if he's out of prison, then he's served his time and made his amends to society. Everyone deserves a second chance, Madison," she chided.

"And *you* don't know that he's made amends!" she hissed back. "For all you know, he broke out of prison."

"So naturally, he comes back to his old stomping grounds and visits a crowded mall that has security cameras everywhere." Happy's whispery voice dripped with sarcasm. "You're right, Madison. Definitely a jail break."

Madison ignored her mother's mockery. "Why on *Earth* did you give that man my phone number!" she complained.

They continued to bicker as they paid for their purchases and made their way back into the main corridor of the mall. Madison insisted the man was a felon, while her mother preached forgiveness and love for mankind.

All too soon, Madison remembered that things had always been this way between her and her mother. Both of her parents were entirely too gullible and too laid-back for their own good. No wonder they hadn't wanted to raise a child. Parenthood meant taking responsibility for someone else's safety and well-being, something her parents barely managed for themselves.

"Oh, look," Happy pointed, as they merged with the steady stream of shoppers. "There's Tom, over at that jewelry store. Maybe he's robbing it. Should we call the mall cops?" She batted her eyes for innocent appeal.

The name of the store caught Madison's eye. *Premium Jewels.* "No, but maybe we should check out the store. I've heard a lot about it recently."

"What about our dinner reservations?"

"We don't have any, Mother. I just said that to get you away from that man."

Happy's sudden stop caused a ripple effect on the steady swarm of people behind them. Someone bumped into her as she stared at the daughter and sputtered, "And now you want to follow him into that store! You are not making any sense at all, Madison Josephine."

"You only call me by my full name when you're mad at me."

"You only call me *Mother* when you're mad at me."

Side by side, Madison Josephine and Mother walked stiffly into the jewelry store.

Tom Haskell was slouched in front of a bracelet display, his large body practically sprawled across the sparkling glass top. He looked away from the pretty sales clerk and smirked when he saw Madison. "Fancy meeting you ladies here," he drawled.

"I've heard so much about this store, I just had to pop in," Madison said, her smile a bit too bright. She spotted the display of men's watches and headed straight to them, even though it meant essentially brushing against Tom Haskell's ink-embellished skin to get there.

"I thought you had dinner reservations," he taunted.

Madison indicated the watch on her wrist. "This silly thing is so old, it doesn't work half the time. All the more reason to shop for a new one."

Torn between which customer to wait on, it didn't take long for the woman to decide Madison was the better bet, particularly when her commission was the ante. She murmured something to the bald man and approached Madison with a smile. "May I show you a watch, perhaps? The ladies watches are just to your left."

"I like these," Madison said decidedly, tapping on the glass. "So will my boyfriend."

"Why, yes, of course." Unlocking the case, she rattled off a long list of attributes for the watches. Presenting a tray for Madison's inspection, she finished with a bright smile. "You simply can't go wrong with any of these. They have been tremendously popular!"

"Yes, I know. Several of my friends purchased these for their husbands."

"Oh, how wonderful. Say, don't I know you from somewhere?"

Madison shook her head, allowing her hair to fall over her face just a bit. "I've never been in the store before."

"Hmm. You just look so familiar..."

Madison quickly turned the topic away from herself. "My boyfriend really liked the watch a friend of ours bought, but I'm not sure which one it is... Do you keep records of your customers, by chance?"

"Well, of course, but those are highly confidential."

Madison pretended to be indecisive. "I think it was that one." She pointed at a gold-plated watch with a shiny face. "No, wait, the bronze one. ... Or was it that one? Oh, shoot, I don't remember! And I would hate to spend this kind of money on the wrong one."

"We have a very generous return policy," the saleswoman offered. "Keep the original receipt and the original packaging, and you can return or exchange your purchase within twenty-one days."

Madison tried to look forlorn. "I just don't want him disappointed on Christmas morning..."

"I think I can say with confidence, ma'am, that no man would be disappointed with any of these fine choices. Did I mention they all are crafted with precision Swiss mechanisms?"

"I don't know..." Madison mimicked the whine she often heard in her daughter's voice. "There was one in particular he wanted, and I just don't remember..."

With a snort of derision, Tom Haskell ambled off to a display on the far side of the store. He was no more likely to buy a gemstone necklace than he was a pricey bracelet, but it didn't stop an eager young salesman from trying to sell him one.

Satisfied that no one could overhear, Madison leaned in and asked, "Isn't there any way you could peek at the records and tell me which watch my friend bought?"

"I'm afraid that's against store policy. Customer files are confidential." Her words said no, but her demeanor said otherwise.

"I understand," Madison said, reaching for the strap of her purse. It looked quite natural when she dropped the whole shebang onto the floor, particularly when she laughed at her own clumsiness. She bent to retrieve it, using exaggerated arm movements. She came back up with a sheepish smile. "I'm such a klutz!" Still smiling, she spoke through her teeth in a low tone no one could overhear. "I dropped a twenty, and I think it slid under your counter. You might want to check after I leave."

The saleswoman didn't miss a beat. "Why, certainly," she beamed. "I would be happy to check on that delivery date for you, ma'am. What did you say the name was?"

Madison wasn't about to tip her hand. She merely wanted to know if anyone on staff could be bribed, and now she had her answer. She popped out the first name that came to mind. "Joan Smith," she said. "From Riverton."

It came as no surprise when the saleswoman returned several minutes later, wearing a frown. There was nothing under that name in their records. Could it possibly be under Damien Smith?

"No, it would be Joan. Maybe I was wrong. Maybe she didn't buy it here." When her phone binged with a message from Bethani, it gave her the perfect out. "Oops, gotta go. I'll check with Joan before I come back in. Thanks, anyway."

Not one to be bothered with the trappings of expensive jewelry, her mother had wandered out to explore the art kiosk in the middle of the mall. Hurrying toward her, from the corner of her eye, Madison saw Tom Haskell slink his way back toward the pretty saleswoman. The clerk had come out from behind the display case and was straightening a stack of pamphlets on a nearby counter. No doubt, she would soon swoop down and retrieve the promised twenty.

Madison grinned as she imagined the woman's irritation when she picked it up. Her parents had given her an entire stack of them. At first glance, it looked like a true twenty-dollar bill, but the back was covered with Bible verses, and instead of Andrew Jackson's portrait, it boasted the image of Jesus Christ.

Oops.

14

"Brash, I think I know what's going on!" Madison called him from the restaurant parking lot, eager to share her discovery with the lawman. "I just came from *Premium Jewels*, and I think I have it figured out."

There was a long pause on the other end of the line. Madison had no idea that he misconstrued her statement to mean she knew about the engagement ring. He finally managed a strangled, "Ahhh…"

"You were right, it's an inside job," she continued excitedly. "I think the salesclerk is calling an accomplice every time a sizable purchase is made by someone from our area. They must know there's a portion of the highway between here and home that's isolated and rather desolate. If they can't stop the shoppers along the highway when they leave town, they go to their houses. They have the addresses in their files. It's the only explanation I can think of."

"I wondered the same thing, but how does that explain them stopping you? You didn't shop at the jewelry store. And neither did Ted Berlin, the other motorist." He conveniently omitted his own roadside robbery, even though he fit the jewelry-store profile.

Madison was quiet for a moment as she considered other theories. "Okay, how about this? Stopping motorists on the roadside has nothing to do with the jewelry store. Those could be random crimes of opportunities. At this time of year, it's a safe bet that people have been out Christmas shopping and have presents in their car."

"Yes, I've considered that theory," Brash agreed.

"But the jewelry store angle still makes sense. The sales-clerk alerts her partner when a big piece of jewelry goes out the door. He goes to the address she gives him and breaks in. A pretty sweet set-up, if you ask me."

"A possible theory, but we need proof. We need to know who her partner is."

"I think I have a lead on that. We ran into an old friend of my parents today. He looks like a rough character. I saw him at the jewelry store, talking rather cozily to the saleswoman involved in the burglaries."

"How do you know which saleswoman it is?"

"Because I bribed her to give me information."

"You did what?!" Brash exploded.

"Calm down, calm down. I didn't *exactly* bribe her. At least not with real money." She hurriedly explained what happened. "But if the woman was willing to break company policy and share private information with me for a measly twenty-dollar bill, imagine what she would tell someone like Tom Haskell for a much bigger profit!"

"Wait a minute. Did you just say Tom Haskell?"

"Yes. You know him?"

"Every lawman in the state of Texas knows Tom Haskell. Or of him. The man is a notorious criminal. The question is, how do *you* know him?"

"He's the old friend my mother ran into."

"Why are your parents friends with the likes of *that man?*" he practically spat. "He was just released from prison. He was serving a fifteen-year sentence for organized criminal activity, but got out early for good behavior."

"They know him from back in the day. I told you, Brash, my father has a very colorful past."

"Criminal, or colorful? Are you sure you haven't gotten the two confused?"

"Colorful," Madison insisted. "But that's not to say he didn't know his share of unsavory characters. Apparently, this Tom Haskell was one of them."

"You stay away from Haskell, Maddy. I don't want you anywhere near that man."

"And I don't want to be near him, but I may not have a choice. Happy invited him for dinner."

Brash exploded again. Once he quietened down, she ventured to add, "It gets worse. She gave him my cell number. I know, I know. We had a big fight about it. Believe me, I am no happier about it than you are. I didn't like the way he leered at me." She shivered just thinking about it.

"Leered?"

Even though he could not see the gesture, she nodded her head. "Like he knew a secret about me, like what color of underwear I was wearing or something."

"He made a pass at you? I swear, I will haul his butt into jail and charge him with harassment!" Brash roared.

"No, it wasn't like that. It wasn't sexual. It was creepier than that. Underwear was a bad example. It was more like he knew the password to my bank account, and planned to use it." She made a smirking noise and added, "For all the good that would do him."

"I still don't like it."

"He knew I wasn't happy with my mother for inviting him over. Hopefully, nothing will come of it and he'll lose my number."

"And Allen Wynn really is Santa Claus."

"Many more of Genny's cookies, and he'll give the old elf a real run for the money," Madison predicted. "I'm sorry, but I need to go. Happy and the kids are already inside and someone has to keep Blake from ordering everything on the menu. I just wanted to share with you what I learned today. At least one of the salespeople at *Premium Jewels* can be bribed, so that could be the link we're looking for."

"Did you catch her name?"

"Danielle."

"Ah, the plot thickens. Danielle just happens to be from Naomi."

"Really? You've already checked her out?"

Before he implicated himself as another of the victims, Brash evaded a direct answer. "I paid a visit to the store manager. There were a few too many coincidences for my comfort. Good work, babe, sorting out the bad apple."

"Why thank you, kind sir. So, what are we going to do next?"

"You're going to go inside the restaurant and order something to eat. Then you're going to text me when you leave town. If you're not home exactly fifty-five minutes after that, I'm coming to look for you."

"I meant about the case."

"So did I. You're going to eat dinner and let me worry about this. End of discussion."

She crinkled her nose and shook her head, neither of which Brash could see. Appearing to give in, she said, "If you think so."

"I know so, Maddy. Say it with me. Brash will take it from here. Come on. Brash will—"

"—take it from here." She rolled her eyes. They both knew it was an empty statement, but if he felt better hearing it aloud, she would indulge him. "Gotta go. Love you."

"Love you, too, sweetheart. Watch your rear-view mirror, call me if you think anyone is tailing you, and let me know the minute you get home."

"Will do, Cap'n. Love you, too." She hung up and finished with the sentiment she had suppressed earlier. "And when I get done with dinner, I'll take it up again, too."

Brash rubbed his eyes, which were now strained and bloodshot. Watching hours of grainy footage from the jewelry store video had also given him a headache, to go along with the eyestrain.

He was tempted to let Maddy go through the video. Not only would it relieve him of the duty, but she had a sharp eye for detail. Sharp enough, he knew, to quickly pick him out from the crowd and note the shiny diamond ring he had purchased. It would ruin the surprise he had planned for

Christmas morning. Plus, she would want to see the ring. And that, in itself, posed a completely different set of problems.

Even if he managed to get the ring back, it probably wouldn't be in the next six days. He didn't want to go down on bended knee without a ring to back up the proposal. Maddy was a practical and understanding woman, but that was asking too much. And it hardly meshed with the fairytale that kept rolling around in his head.

He needed another ring.

In the meantime, he watched more video. He saw Marilyn Bashinski come into the store and make her way to the watch display. A young male clerk patiently pulled out each watch for her perusal and eventually closed the sale. Brash scanned the shot for anyone unusual roaming around in the background, but saw nothing amiss.

Now that he knew to look for him, Brash detected Tom Haskell on the video feed. The known felon came into the store on three different occasions and each time, he went directly to Danielle's station. The two would have a brief conversation and then the big man would leave.

There seemed nothing unusual about the exchanges, but Brash rewound each occurrence a dozen times, freezing frames and taking notes. He recorded the time and duration of each visit. Tried to zoom in enough to read lips. Noticed the people in the background and the counters where they stood. Watched Danielle's behavior after her visitor left. It was wishful thinking on his part, hoping for a telltale pattern in her actions. Nothing jumped out at him.

He even made note of Danielle's actions after making a sale. He never saw her make covert phone calls or send text messages. He never saw her search through store records or jot down notes.

Throughout the hours of video, he had noted several young couples come into the store and shyly look at engagement rings. He spotted the blond woman Danielle spoke of, the one who kept her eye on a particular ring. He even saw the man who purchased the ring, and hoped it was her boyfriend, or else she would be devastated. He saw her hopeful face the day she came in and discovered the ring was gone.

It took two days, but after hours of watching the videos, Brash came to a conclusion. If Danielle Applegate—or any of the other employees, for that matter—was guilty of exploiting customer purchases, she was doing so off camera. He could see nothing amiss.

His own face was one of the last images caught on tape. Why, he wondered, did he look so nervous? He loved Madison more than he ever thought possible. He harbored no doubts about wanting to share his life with her. So why did he look as skittish and frightened as some of those college kids on the security tapes?

Ignoring his pale image on film, Brash perused the background for someone paying him undue attention. Other than an occasional person who pointed to him in recognition, either from the television show or his own football career, no one seemed particularly impressed as he made the most important purchase of his life. Again, nothing appeared to be amiss.

When the screen finally went blank, Brash heaved out a relieved sigh. He rubbed his eyes again and stretched his broad shoulders. He knew he would need to watch the footage at least once again, to pick up on anything he had missed the first time.

But not tonight.

Tonight, he had a much greater task in mind. He knew this was the reason he looked so nervous on the video. The reason his hands still perspired when he thought about it.

Tonight, he planned to ask permission to marry Maddy.

He dressed in newly starched jeans and a blue chambray western shirt that played well against the chocolate of his eyes. His hair was newly trimmed, his face shaved clean. After sliding on ostrich-skin boots and belt, he added a splash of his favorite cologne and studied himself in the mirror. He wasn't a vain man, but he supposed he was decent-enough looking to catch a woman's eyes. His stomach was still flat and his chest still broad and muscled. In his line of work, he had to stay in shape. Other than a rogue knee that popped its protest now and then, he was still in excellent physical condition.

He had noticed a few more gray strands of late, weaving their way through his dark-auburn hair. Maddy claimed they made him look dignified. Megan teased him about going bald, but his thick shock of hair was as full as ever, even dusted with gray. Just shy of forty-three, Brash wanted to believe he was still in his prime.

When Megan saw him, she gave him a sharp once over and, eventually, a thumb's up. "Looking sharp, Dad. What's the occasion?"

"Dinner with Maddy's parents. Are you ready?"

The teen looked down at her stylish but ripped jeans. A cute top and her favorite Sticker Pierce cowboy boots, personally autographed by the legend himself, completed her ensemble. "I may not look it next to you, but I'm ready."

"You look beautiful, as always," her father assured her. "Don't think I haven't noticed all those boys hanging around you these days. I keep beating them off with a stick, but one day, one of them is bound to get through and ask you out on a date."

"Da-ad!" Behind her large-framed glasses—red, for the holidays—the teenager rolled her eyes.

"Can't help it, Meg. I'm not ready for my little girl to be such a gorgeous young woman."

"You can't hold back the hands of time, you know."

"I can try." He brushed a kiss into her hair as he opened the truck door and helped her inside. "And remember, a gentleman should always open the door for a lady. If a boy doesn't offer to open your door, don't bother getting in his car." He paused and amended his statement. "Come to think of it, you don't need to be getting into a boy's car yet, anyway. Ask to ride a bike."

"Cool! A motorcycle?" Her eyes danced with merriment.

"No! A bicycle. Better yet, a tricycle."

Megan rolled her eyes again as Brash closed her door and came around to get into the driver's seat.

"At least these are Bethani's cool grandparents, and not the stuck-up ones," Megan remarked as he started the motor. "I don't look forward to meeting that set."

Secretly, Brash agreed. He, too, dreaded the day he had to meet Charles and Annette Reynolds. From everything Maddy had told him about her former in-laws, he already had a dismal opinion of them. He doubted they would ever approve of him, not when he was competing with their sainted son. It would be tough enough, gaining Bethani's approval to marry her mother.

That worry occupied his thoughts as he drove the rest of the way to the Big House.

After dinner, Brash managed to get Charlie alone for a talk.

"I know you don't know me very well, sir, and I know Madison is a grown woman, but I believe in doing things the traditional way. I'd like to ask for your blessing to propose to your daughter."

Charlie's blue eyes twinkled as he studied the younger man.

It was true, he didn't know him well, but everyone knew who Brash deCordova was. He was one of The Sisters' golden sons. Star athlete and honor student back in the day, professional football player and coach in his first career, now honorable police chief and special investigator for the county. From a father's point of view, he was the man who put the sparkle back into his daughter's eyes, perhaps brighter than ever before.

That didn't mean Charlie Cessna would make it easy for him, however. Normally a confident man, Brash looked particularly vulnerable at the moment. Charlie couldn't help but tease the lawman.

"And if I don't give you permission?" Charlie asked.

Brash's deep voice was steady, yet firm. "With all due respect, sir, I didn't ask for permission. I asked for your blessing."

Charlie threw back his blond head and laughed. "I'm just messing with you. You have both! Welcome to the family, son!" he boomed in delight.

Brash couldn't help but frown. "I plan to surprise her at Christmas, so I'd appreciate you keeping your voice down."

Charlie looked dutifully chastised. He tiptoed across the room and jovially slapped Brash on the back. In a loud whisper, he repeated, "Welcome to the family, my son! You are the best thing that's ever happened to my little girl, besides those two kids of hers."

"I appreciate that, sir. I plan to do everything in my power to always make her happy."

"I think this calls for a beer, don't you? Sit down, take a load off, and relax. You look like you could use a cold one 'bout now."

Brash wouldn't argue. He had been more nervous than he thought he would be.

And this was the easy one, he reminded himself.

When Charlie returned with two frosty longnecks, Brash drank half the bottle and made small talk, before working the conversation around to Tom Haskell.

"Yep, I've known Tom on and off through the years. I first met him when we were out in Colorado, dealing for casinos. He had hooked up with a gal from here and brought her out to work the faro tables. Allie and I were out there, working blackjack and roulette. They needed a place to stay, so we put them up for a few weeks, until they could find their own place. Years later, we had a brief stint together in the trucking industry. Last time I saw him, he was running books out in Vegas with a new woman by his side."

"What woman was he with from here?" Brash asked.

Charlie squinted his eyes as he tried to recall her name. "I think her name was Mary." He took another long swallow of his beer. "She made a play for me one evening, and I tossed her out on her ear. I've done a lot of things over the years, some I'm not too proud of. Folks have called me a lot of different things, too, some that I deserved, some that I didn't. But one thing they have to call me is faithful. It's the true measure of a man, son." He leveled Brash a long look. "If a man can't be faithful to his wife, he's no man at all."

"I agree completely. That's one thing you'll never have to worry about with me, sir. My first marriage ended in divorce, but it ended in honor. I never betrayed my vows."

In reply, Charlie tipped his bottle to Brash.

Life lesson over, Charlie continued down memory lane. "Yep, ole Tom always had a thing for gambling," he said. "I hear after Vegas, he branched out on his own. Ran a big operation back here in Texas. Heard it landed him in Huntsville for a nickel."

"Should have been fifteen, but he got out early. Good behavior, they called it, even though the prison bars never held him back. Far as I know, he's still in business."

"Allie is too innocent for her own good," Charlie said with a frown. "She sees the good in everyone. Lucky for me, but not always good for her own safety. She can't see a rotten apple in a barrel, even when they're stinking up the whole bunch."

"This Mary gal you mentioned. You remember her last name?"

"Something common, I think. Allie might remember, but as far as I was concerned, she was forgettable, even before that night."

The women came in from the kitchen, their sleeves damp from doing dishes.

"I kept telling Mom I had a dishwasher—two, in fact—but she insisted on doing the dishes by hand," Madison laughed.

"You have no idea what a luxury it is, being able to use all that hot, sudsy water. After some of the places we've lived, doing dishes by hand here is a real treat."

"Who would like dessert?" Madison asked. "The Cookie Campaign starts in about ten minutes, but we have time for dessert. Genny left a buttermilk pie."

"Too bad she and that hunk of a boyfriend of hers couldn't be here tonight," Allie said. She was quite open about the harmless little crush she had on Cutter.

"They were having their Fire Department Christmas Party tonight. Dad? Brash? Pie?"

"A double piece, honey," her father said. "With a big scoop of Bluebell Homemade Vanilla. We can't get that in Africa, you know."

"Brash?"

"Uh, I promised Megan I'd take her for a snow cone. They opened for the holidays, you know. Frosty Ice Palace, they're calling it. I thought the twins might want to go along."

"Hey, that sounds good. I might join you."

"Don't you need to be here to pass out cookies?"

For once, Charlie was attuned to someone else's plight. He saw the nervous glint in Brash's eye and suspected the cause. "Yeah, honey, stay here with your mom and I and help us out. You saw me out there last night. I didn't know when to shut it off. I need you to keep me on track."

With a bit of a scowl, Madison agreed. "Well, okay, I guess."

"I'll bring you back a surprise," Brash promised. He brushed a kiss across her lips and was out of the room before she could utter a comeback.

15

The *Frosty Ice* trailer sat under a canopy of Christmas lights and was surrounded by huge illuminated snow-flakes. Christmas music blared from speakers set among a collection of inflatable snowmen. Picnic tables were covered in white to imitate recent snowfall.

If not for the warm temperatures, the atmosphere might have been more convincing.

Brash chose a table as far from the other patrons as possible.

"There's Tabitha and Penny Jo," Megan said, waving at her friends. "Can we invite them over?"

"Not just yet. I want to talk to you three for a minute."

"Uh-oh," Megan said, rolling her eyes in jest. "I got the rundown earlier. Blake, it is always polite to open the door for a girl. Beth, never get into a guy's car unless he opens your door for you. The exception is if he drives a souped-up motor-cycle." Her eyes twinkled as she teased her father.

"Excellent points, but that's not what this is about," Brash said. He toyed with the crushed ice in his cup. "I wanted to talk to you guys about Christmas."

"It will be here in five days," Blake observed smartly.

"Yeah, I heard." Brash dug his plastic spoon into the ice, watching as red syrup pooled into the hole. His heart bled much the same. This was tougher than he imagined. "The thing is, I, uh, I have a special gift I want to give Maddy. And I want to make sure all of you are okay with it."

Megan's eyes glowed as she bounced up and down on the bench in excitement. "It's a ring, isn't it?" she guessed. "You're going to propose to their mom!"

Brash glanced first at Blake, then at his twin sister. "I want to. If I have your blessing."

"Are you kidding me? Of course it's okay with us!" Blake answered, his face aglow.

As he and Megan exchanged high fives, Brash noticed that Bethani remained silent. His heart froze in his chest. "Beth?" he managed to ask.

The teen didn't quite meet his eyes.

"This is so cool, Beth!" Megan insisted. "We'll be sisters!"

"Maybe," she mumbled, shrugging one shoulder.

"I love your mother, Bethani," Brash said, his voice now strong and sure. "And I love you and Blake. I want the five of us to be a family. Megan, you, Blake, your mom, and me."

"You didn't stay married the first time," Bethani pointed out.

Brash made no apologies. "You're right, I didn't. Megan and I have talked about this. Her mother and I loved each other, but not in the way a husband and wife should have. We were all wrong for each other, and too young to realize it. If we had stayed married, we would have ended up hating one another. Everyone, including Megan, would have been miserable. As it is, Shannon is married to my best friend, and she's now one of my closest friends, too. And I will always have a special place in my heart for her. Together, she and I made an amazing daughter." He smiled indulgently at a misty-eyed Megan before continuing, "Just like your mom will always have a special place in her heart for your father, because he gave her you and Blake. But that's the cool thing about love. There's always room for more."

"How do you know you won't find room for someone else? Someone instead of my mom?"

"Because I love your mom in a way I've never loved anyone else, not even Shannon."

Bethani looked at her best friend, accusation in her eyes. "How can you let him talk about your mom that way?" she challenged.

"He's not talking bad about my mom, Beth," Megan pointed out in a soft voice. "He's talking pretty wonderful about yours."

Bethani's lower lip trembled. "But you're being disloyal to your mother!"

"No, I'm not. I was still little when they broke up, but I remember the fights. They weren't happy back then. Now they are. And you aren't being disloyal to your dad," she said perceptively, "by giving your blessing to make your mom happy again."

"It—It feels like it," Bethani whispered, fighting back tears.

Brash broke in with a firm but gentle voice. "Your dad is gone, Bethani. I'm sorry about that, but it's the way it is. But I'm here, and I want to make a life with your mom. I'll be good to her, and I'll be good to you and Blake. I'll take care of you the best way I know how, the same way I take care of Megan. I want us to be a family."

Blake already knew his position. "I'm in. I haven't seen Mom this happy in a long time. If it's up to me, we'll marry you."

"Thank you, Blake. That means the world to me." Brash clasped Blake's hand and held on. After a moment of bonding, he turned back toward the boy's twin sister. "Bethani? Will you have me?"

Sniffing away tears, she bumped her shoulder into her dark-haired friend. "I always did want a sister," she admitted. She slowly lifted her eyes to Brash's. "You can ask her. If she says it's okay, I guess it's okay with me, too."

A weight lifted from Brash's heart and he let out a boyish whoop. "I gotta admit, you had me sweating there for a minute, young lady," he said. His stern attitude was a poor cover for his nervousness.

"Yeah, I should have made you sweat it out," she decided with a calculated look in her eyes. "I could have held out for a pony."

"You want a pony? I'll give you a ranch full of them!"

Her eyes lit with intrigue. "That's right; you do have a ranch, don't you? With horses and cows and oil wells!"

"Well, it belongs to the entire deCordova family, but yeah, we do have a ranch. You'll be a part of it now."

"Wait. We don't have to move, do we? Because we just moved into the Big House."

"No, doofus, he'll move in with us," Blake chided his sister. "Right, Mr. de?"

Brash laughed. "I don't know yet. I haven't gotten that far. First, I have to ask your mom to marry me."

"You know she'll say yes."

"Ooh, do I get my own room at the Big House?" Megan wanted to know.

"You could have the other turret!" Bethani volunteered. At the moment, the turret on the far end from hers served as a hangout lounge for their friends. With Blake's room on the second floor, she had the third floor to herself.

As the girls made plans to makeover the room, Blake had other things on his mind. "Does this mean I can go fishing out at the ranch whenever I want? Can I have my own horse? Hey, maybe I could show a steer at the 4-H show this year!"

Brash's laughter rang out in the night air. His heart was full. He had worried for nothing.

Things were going to work out after all.

Back at the Big House, a steady stream of cars filed by to view the twinkling Christmas lights and listen to a recorded message. The luckier ones stopped for a bag of cookies.

"Okay, now remember, I want to surprise her," Brash cautioned the teenagers before they piled from the truck. "No hints."

"Do happy smiles count?" Megan wanted to know.

"Nah, she'll just think you're full of Christmas cheer. Why don't y'all go relieve your elders and take a turn at handing out cookies?" he suggested.

"You just want to hug on our mom," Blake teased. "Smooch a little."

"That, too," Brash admitted.

Bethani put hands over both her ears. "TMI. I'm glad y'all's bedroom will be on a different floor than mine."

"Mine, too," Megan giggled. "Come on, let's go hand out cookies. I see Connor Evans in line!"

Brash parked the truck and watched as the girls raced into the house, giggling and laughing the whole way.

Madison noticed as well and asked about it later, when she and Brash settled in the front parlor with a glass of wine. With the room darkened, they could watch the festivities out on the lawn and enjoy the twinkle of the tree lights. It wasn't complete privacy, but it was enough to snuggle on the small settee in the shadows.

"I don't know what was in those snow cones, but the kids certainly came back in high spirits."

"I'm not sure," Brash frowned, "but I may have promised Bethani a pony for Christmas."

"A *pony*?" Madison hooted.

"Long story. I'll tell you about it sometime."

"How about now?"

"How about we use these few moments of privacy and talk about something else?" he suggested, taking her wine glass from her and setting it on the table.

"How about we don't talk at all?"

"Even better," he murmured, lowering his mouth to hers. Gathering her close, he kissed her long and deep. "I love you, Madison."

"I love you, too. Did I tell you how handsome you look tonight?" She lifted her face to whisper in his ear. "And very sexy, I might add."

"You could wear a feed sack, and still be the sexiest woman I've ever seen."

One kiss led to another, each one deeper and hungrier than the last. "You have no idea how hard it is," Brash muttered against the long, slender column of her throat, "trying to remain a gentleman, when I want you so badly."

Despite his best intentions, his hands began to wander and knead. She shifted slightly away to allow him better access, her own hands greedy.

"Believe me, I know," she breathed. Beneath her agile fingers, the top buttons of his shirt popped open.

"Don't start something we can't finish," he warned through a heated kiss.

"Then you'd better stop touching me like that... nooo, don't stop," she complained, all in the same breathless sentence.

It pained him to say it, but he did. "We have to, Maddy." One more lingering caress, and he stilled his hands. "We've talked about this. We have to set an example for the kids."

"I know, I know," she grumbled. "If we can't control our own raging hormones, how can we expect them to?" Still throbbing with unfulfilled need, Madison blew out an unsteady breath. "I don't like it, but I know."

"I've taken so many cold showers, I think I'm now an honorary Eskimo," Brash admitted on a grumble.

Maddy smiled in response. "At least I'm saving on the expense of hot water. That's something. Not much, but something."

"Here." He thrust her wineglass at her. "Drink your wine and keep your hands off me, before I forget everything I just said and decide to ravish you, after all."

"Do not tempt me," she warned, only half in jest.

"Maybe we should change to a safer topic. Like the case."

"Not as much fun, but I agree. Much safer. So, anything new?" She settled comfortably into the curve of his arm and sipped her wine.

"Your dad said Tom Haskell used to have a girlfriend that lived here. As far as I knew, he was from the Navasota area and didn't really have a history here. But if he has ties to The Sisters, he might be more involved in the gambling ring than I realized."

"Was this anytime recent?"

"No, like in the seventies."

"That was a long time ago, Brash. I'm not sure it would be relevant."

"Maybe not, but it's worth checking out."

"Especially if you can tie him into the Christmas Crimes. You've always wondered if they were related."

"I've watched those security tapes until I'm cross-eyed. I can't see anything suspicious between Tom Haskell and Danielle Applegate."

Madison sat up in interest. "Her last name is Applegate?"

"Yes, that's right. Why, do you know it?"

"That's the name of one of the women Vanessa Hutchins works with. She's in the Bunco group."

"Where does she live?"

"Several miles out of town, out on Luna Road. Her first name is Charmaine."

"They could be related," Brash reasoned. "Growing up, Danielle lived out that direction. She didn't mention whether her parents still live here, but apparently, her aunt does. She's the one who told her about the recent burglaries."

Madison chewed on her inner lip. After a moment of silence, she announced, "So, now I'm even more convinced that Danielle Applegate is involved."

"How so?"

"Vanessa and Charmaine both work at the pharmacy. It's only natural to talk to your co-worker about what you're doing for Christmas, the gifts you're buying and wrapping, that sort of thing."

"It is?"

She ignored the interruption and continued with her theory. "So, what if Vanessa discusses her Christmas purchases at work? I know almost everyone in The Sisters uses Shubert's Pharmacy, being it's the only one in either town. What if Charmaine inadvertently tells Danielle some of the things people are buying this year? Danielle tells Tom Haskell, Tom Haskell breaks into the houses, they share the wealth between them."

"I suppose it's possible."

She could hear the doubt in his voice. "But you don't think it's probable."

"I see some problems with that scenario. For starters, Tom Haskell doesn't fit the description of the man Marilyn Bashinski saw running from her house."

"You're the one who said the man ran a gambling operation from prison. It stands to reason that he has underlings to do the dirty work for him."

"True. But I'm still not convinced that Danielle Applegate is the common denominator in all this. I did a background check on her and she's clean. Not even a speeding ticket. And there's nothing on the surveillance tapes to incriminate her or any of her co-workers from the jewelry store. I hate to say it, but there's also no reason to think Tom Haskell is directly connected to the Christmas Crimes, either."

Disappointment sagged in her voice. "You think I'm way off base. That I'm fixating on the Danielle/Tom Haskell link because I don't like the man."

"Don't get me wrong. I'd love to pin this on the guy, too. And yes, your theory is somewhat plausible, but only if we assume the hijackings along the road are crimes of opportunity and not part of the overall plan. Still possible, but something about it feels off. I think we're still missing something."

"Like what?"

"If I knew that, I'd have already made an arrest."

16

Madison knew she was being stubborn. Brash was an experienced officer of the law and made perfectly valid points to discount her theory about Danielle Applegate and Tom Haskell. There was nothing to point at their guilt. Nothing, other than this nagging notion in the back of her head. Like a hound dog on a scent, she couldn't let it go.

She still tested the theory in her head the next day, as they finished the final round of cookies for the Cookie Campaign.

"Last batch, going in the oven," Granny Bert announced. She dusted her gnarled hands off and propped them upon her hips. "Can't say I'm not glad to be done with it. This was a good project, but I'm getting too old to bake this many cookies on an almost daily basis."

"You, old?" Happy smiled at her mother-in-law with true affection. "You haven't aged a day since I married into this family. You're just not accustomed to being tied down to one task this long."

"I think you have me confused with my son, missy. Charlie is the one who doesn't like doing the same old thing every day."

"True, but I think he may have learned that from his mother. Admit it, baking all these cookies keeps you from doing the things you'd really like to be doing, like traveling, or spending time with your handsome cowboy friend."

"I do like to travel, but not at Christmastime. I like to be here with my family during the holidays." She handily avoided all references to Sticker. "Baking has been fun, but I'm plumb tuckered out from being on my feet for so long. And I still have more shopping to do. Ready or not, Christmas is upon us, girls."

"So, when these cookies are gone, the Cookie Campaign is over?" A note of sorrow clung to Happy's voice. She and Charlie had thoroughly enjoyed the interaction with old friends and new acquaintances.

"Folks will still drive by, looking at the lights," Granny Bert assured her. "But when they text the number, they'll just get a song, or a heartfelt wish for a Merry Christmas. Leaves us these last few evenings to take care of our own rat killing."

"I guess that's only fair," Happy agreed with a sigh. "I know you've been doing this a lot longer than Charlie and I have. Maddy, you and Brash are still going shopping this evening, right?" When her daughter didn't reply, she repeated the question.

"I'm sorry," Madison apologized. "My mind was somewhere else. And yes, ma'am, we're leaving as soon as his shift is over. I don't know the first thing about picking out a rod and reel for Blake."

"You've been quiet all afternoon," Granny Bert remarked. "What's bothering you?"

"I can't stop thinking about the Christmas Crimes. I think I'm on to a good lead, but Brash doesn't fully agree."

"You can run it by me, see if it makes sense to an old lady."

Maddy gave her grandmother a shrewd look. "You aren't fooling me a minute with this 'old lady' routine. You just want in the loop."

"Darn tootin', I do. But you know good and well I can probably help."

After a moment's consideration, Maddy gave in. "Maybe you can help. What can you tell me about a woman named Danielle Applegate? She grew up here before moving to Bryan. I think she might be a niece to Charmaine Applegate, the woman who works at the pharmacy."

"I remember Danielle. And yes, you're right about her being Charmaine's niece, even though they tell a different story. In their version, Charmaine claims to be her mother."

The news took Madison by surprise. "What? Why?"

"Charmaine and her husband took the baby to raise, after her sister gave birth out of wedlock. Right out of high school, Molly met some fellow and took off with him. Next thing we know, Charmaine leaves town for a couple of months, then comes back with a baby, claiming to have been hospitalized in Dallas."

"How do you know that wasn't true?"

"Because your grandfather and I happened to be over in Lufkin, where their momma was originally from. Who do you think we see, but a very trim Charmaine and a very pregnant Molly, just a few weeks before Danielle was born. It didn't take a rocket scientist to know which one was the baby's mother, especially when Molly came back to town and picked up her romance with Randy Redmond, right where she left off. It paid off, too. They were married within six months."

The surprises kept coming. "Danielle's birth mother married a Redmond?"

"Yes, but the marriage didn't last but a few years. When she realized Randy wasn't going to be the next banker in the family, she moved on to greener pastures."

"So, Charmaine raised her niece as her own child and no one was the wiser?"

"Oh, most folks knew their stories didn't add up, but they also knew the child was better off with Charmaine than her sister."

"What happened to the sister?"

"You mean Molly? After dumping Randy, she married Berle Shubert."

This was the biggest surprise of all. "You mean Molly Shubert, the second and much younger wife of sweet Mr. Shubert from the pharmacy? *That's* the Molly we're talking about?"

"The one and only."

"So, Molly Shubert had a baby right out of high school, gave it to her sister to raise, married into and out of the Redmond family, and then hooked up with a man old enough to be her father?"

Granny Bert nodded, her facial expression filled with meaning. "A man whose first wife conveniently died of a prescribed drug overdose. A man who was rich enough, and lonely enough, to buy his young, pretty wife anything her heart desired."

"But—But Mr. Shubert wouldn't harm a fly!" Madison sputtered in outrage. "You can't seriously think he had something to do with his first wife's death!"

"Never said that he did. But Charmaine has been a tech at that pharmacy her whole career. What's more, she got a job there for her sister, about a year before Blanche Shubert took a fatal overdose."

"Are you saying what I think you're saying?"

"I'm saying that Molly Crowder Redmond set her sights on Berle Shubert and she didn't rest until she had his two-carat ring on her finger. I'm saying she befriended Blanche and somehow ingratiated herself into their lives. Ran errands and cooked for her as Blanche started getting weaker. I'm saying she practically pushed her way into the house, all the while pushing their two daughters out. She even convinced Berle to let her plan a surprise trip for Blanche to celebrate their fortieth anniversary. I'm saying that Molly was one of the last people to see Blanche alive, and the first person in the house when she died. By the time the daughters asked questions and the police got around to investigating—that hair-brained Roy Lee Sikes was chief at the time—the pill bottles were long gone. I'm telling you that four months after his wife was buried—four months, mind you!—Berle Shubert married that girl down in Tahiti, on a trip he thought was meant for Blanche."

Madison was horrified by her grandmother's account. "That's awful! And the police could never prove anything?"

Granny Bert snorted, resorting to one of her favorite sayings. "Sikes was as useless as a screen door on a submarine! That man couldn't prove it was raining during a flash flood. The daughters tried to bring in outside investigators, but

Berle wouldn't hear of it. Threatened to cut them out of the will. The way I hear it, Molly managed to do so anyway, although I'm not sure they know it yet. That should make for an interesting situation when old Berle dies. He's been doing poorly, you know. Too sick to even play Santa this year. Not sure if his diabetes is catching up with him, or if Molly's got eyes on another husband."

Scowling heavily, Madison asked, "Granny, are you sure about all this?"

The look her grandmother seared her with could wither a rose. "What kind of question is that?"

Madison shook her head in defeat. "A silly one, I'm sure."

"So why are you asking about Charmaine and Danielle? Molly may be a real number, but as far as I know, Charmaine is a decent kind of gal."

The buzzer sounded on the oven. Happy donned a mitt and pulled the trays out, leaving Granny Bert and Madison to their conversation. Without calling Tom Haskell's name, Madison briefly outlined her theory.

"I don't know," Granny Bert ruminated. "Seems like a mighty flimsy connection to me."

"It makes sense," Madison insisted stubbornly. "Almost all the cases involve a jewelry purchase. Working at the jewelry store, Danielle knows where the people live and what they bought. That gives her means and opportunity. And believe me, the man she's friendly with is definitely not above breaking into their homes to steal it."

"Has this same sort of thing happened with customers in other towns?"

"Not that Brash is aware of."

"I hate to point out the obvious, but there are very few millionaires, if any, living here in Juliet and Naomi. The bigger diamonds and the really valuable jewels are most likely under trees in some other town. Why pick only on customers living in The Sisters?"

"Like Brash pointed out, we live in a trusting community. Not many houses here have alarm systems. Half of those are only used when the owners are away on vacation. A few people still don't even bother locking their homes or automobiles. He thinks all that trust and sense of security makes our town an easy target."

"Hate to say it, but he might have a point."

"Being from here originally, Danielle Applegate would know that."

"True, but so would plenty of other people."

Happy interrupted them with an exasperated, "Am I going to get any help over here?"

"Sorry, Mom," Madison apologized, quickly lending her mother a hand. As they worked to transfer cookies to cooling racks and sort those already cooled, Madison thought about all she had learned.

"I still can't believe that about Molly Shubert," she said after a while. "She seems so refined. I only know her from the pharmacy, but she always seems nice."

"It's easy to be nice and to put on airs," Granny Bert pointed out, "when you're spending someone else's money. Berle's credit card bought her way into the finest salons and spas, where they whittled away the rough edges and polished her up nice and pretty. But that old bird still has some sharp talons. Did I mention she has a connection to your friend Bernie Havlicek?"

Madison's eyes widened and she stopped in the middle of bagging a cookie assortment. "How?"

"Her other daughter married Bernie's younger brother. Like most of his family, Doug had an aversion to working. He was more creative than most of his relatives, though, and he was forever coming up with some get-rich-quick scheme. He even convinced Molly to invest in a hotshot service. The business lasted longer than the marriage did. She keeps it on the down low, but the way I hear it, Molly still has her fingers in the business. Now that she's got money, she likes to downplay her connection to the Havliceks."

"What's a hotshot service?" Madison asked.

To her surprise, her mother was the one to answer that question. "That's what your father did for a while. It's an on-call delivery service, geared mostly for the oil industry. When something breaks down on an oilrig, it can mean losing thousands of dollars an hour. People will pay ungodly amounts to have a piece of equipment delivered onsite. I've seen your father drive all the way out to Odessa to pick up some critical gear and deliver it to a rig over in Jasper." She made a tsk-tsk sound and shook her head in wonder. "He wore out a brand-new Dodge truck, driving back and forth across Texas."

"Is that what you called his trucking days? I thought you meant he drove an eighteen-wheeler."

Her mother shook her head, long hair dancing around her shoulders. "He took the smaller jobs, when a half-ton truck was faster and more efficient. Plus, using his own truck meant less paperwork and regulations. And you know your father, the less restrictions, the better!" Happy laughed at her own joke.

"Never did like my son working for those people," Granny Bert grumbled. "Those Havliceks are nothing but trouble!"

"Wait. Dad worked for the Havliceks?" The thought was preposterous.

"Only for a few months," her mother assured her. "He made a couple of runs with Tom Haskell—they were both working as hotshots at the time—but something just didn't feel right to him. He suspected they were carrying stolen goods. He put in his resignation right after that."

"A prime example," Granny Bert spat, "of the sort of riff-raff those Havliceks mingle with."

"I think my head is going to explode," Madison murmured in amazement. "I have learned all sorts of new things in the last thirty minutes."

"Well, here's something else to tuck into your little noggin," her grandmother said. "Something you can pass on to your man. Word is that there's another game scheduled for tomorrow night, the last one of the year. They're calling it a Christmas party so the wives won't grumble about the men going out, so close to the holidays."

Madison's heart rate kicked up a notch. This might be the break Brash was hoping for. "Really? Where?"

"That's the sketchy part. I couldn't get a firm location, but I heard Doug and Bernie were hosting it."

Happy stared at her mother-in-law, a look of confusion and awe upon her face. "How do you even know that?" she cried.

Madison laughed, squeezing her mother's shoulders as she headed for the door. "I gave up asking a long time ago. Can you two take it from here? I have to call Brash!"

17

Three hours later, Madison and Brash strolled through the mall, arm in arm.

"Are you sure you didn't mind coming tonight?" she asked again. "I would have understood if you took a raincheck."

"There's no time for rainchecks," Brash told her with a rueful smile. "Christmas is four days away. It was now or never."

"Still, I would have understood. Catching criminals is more important than catching fish."

"Not to a sixteen-year-old. I was happy to help you choose a rod and reel for Blake. He's going to love it."

"Help? You picked it out all by yourself. I don't know the first thing about spin-casts and open-face reels and all that other Greek stuff you were spewing. It's all a foreign language, as far as I'm concerned."

"You'll learn," he chuckled. "Just like I've had to learn the difference between flat gloss and glossy gloss, and mouse vs. styling gel, and all that teenage-girl jargon."

"Plain English," Madison assured him. When her phone binged, she pulled it from her pocket and studied it with a frown. "Speaking of teenage girls, the one I own was sweet enough to install a bunch of new apps on my phone. I now get an alert every five minutes, telling me about the latest sale. Hard as it is to imagine, all those sale items just happen to be on my daughter's very extensive Christmas list."

"Go figure." Brash laughed at her exasperated expression before suggesting, "Can't you just delete the apps?"

"If I were smart enough to operate my smartphone, I would!" she retorted.

"We can look at it over dinner."

"Are you sure you have time to eat? We can grab something to go and eat in the car. I know you'd rather be working on the gambling case right now."

"That is where you are wrong." He squeezed the hand tucked into the crook of his elbow. "There is nowhere I'd rather be than here with you. My officers have eyes on the Havlicek brothers, and Cutter volunteered to help keep an eye on a few of the other known players. If they're setting up a game, we'll see it."

They reached the entrance to the restaurant, where Brash paused in the doorway. "How often do you and I get to eat out, just the two of us? I know this isn't a fancy candlelight dinner, but at least it's just you and me."

"My favorite dinner combination," Madison smiled, lightly brushing against him as she slipped past his outstretched arm.

The hostess showed them to a booth, where they settled upon the same bench seat. Like teenagers on a date, they held hands as they waited for their meal to arrive. Brash declared all talk about work off limits. Tonight was for talking about the holidays and the kids and things that didn't revolve around police work.

When her phone binged again, Madison took action. "Okay, I am deleting these silly apps. Like this one for *TossUp*. That silly thing bings when I get within so many feet of the store. I have no idea how it knows where I am, but it's a little bit spooky." She scrolled through the options. "Why on Earth do they need access to my microphone and location, anyway?"

Brash's mischievous grin was boyishly handsome. "To bing you when you get near a store and lure you inside."

"No, thanks. Bye-bye, *TossUp*." She jabbed the delete button. "You, too, *Shop Goddess*."

"What about that one for *Tasty's?*"

"I actually like that place. I guess I'll leave it," Madison decided. "They have some sort of loyalty program. Show your phone at checkout and it counts toward a free drink."

"Speaking of drinks, here are ours."

"Perfect." With a bright smile, Madison tucked her phone away and leaned into his arm. "No kids, no pesky bings from my phone, no shop talk. Just you and me."

"Sounds like a definite winner."

After a relaxed meal, they shopped at one last store before calling it a night. Piling their purchases into his truck, Madison smiled triumphantly. "I am officially through with my Christmas shopping, and it's still four days before Christmas! Yay, me."

"Now to wrap it all," he reminded her, helping her inside and shutting the door behind her.

"Kill joy." She shot daggers at him with her laughing eyes.

"I'll make it up to you by buying you a caramel latte."

Madison did her best queen imitation. "For a Caramel Crazy Latte, you are forgiven, my humble and lowly servant."

She granted the playful reprieve, using the tip of her nail as her royal specter.

His dark eyes danced with amusement. "Thank you, your highness."

Several minutes later, he noticed how quiet she had become. "Is something wrong?" he asked.

"Just thinking."

"About what?"

"I can't say."

"Why not?"

She bit her lower lip. "You said the topic was off limits."

He made a sound that was half grumble, half snort. "You might as well say what's on your mind. We're obviously both still thinking about it."

He didn't have to make the offer twice. She turned to him and blurted out her thoughts. "What you said earlier, calling me your highness. It reminded me of that time in the cave, when Derron and I were tied up. That's what the big boss called me. That's always bothered me."

"That bothers you? Because a drug lord thinks you're a snob?" he asked, surprised.

"No! I couldn't care less what a drug dealer thinks of me. What bothers me is that there's someone else who calls me that. Someone who would be more than happy to see harm come my way."

"You're talking about Barry Redmond." It wasn't a question, but a flat, harsh statement.

"I know, I know. He's an upstanding member of society. Part of the founding family of Naomi. President of the bank. It's a crazy notion to think he might be messed up with a drug operation... Isn't it?" She added the last in a small voice.

To her surprise, Brash's voice was low and a bit rough. "I don't know," he admitted. "To tell you the truth, I've considered it, more than once. I know his ex-wife took the blame for most of what happened this fall, but I'm not so sure she was the only one at fault. There have been too many things that didn't add up. And banker or not, Barry seems to have a free flow of cash these days. He's going through women and money at a staggering rate."

"I saw his latest new car," Madison agreed with a nod. "And the new girlfriend. I heard she was a swimsuit model."

"I heard she was the sort of model who didn't bother with the swimsuit."

Madison wrinkled her nose in distaste, choosing to change the topic. "Hey, guess what? I just learned today that Molly Shubert was once married to Randy Redmond."

"So I hear. I guess that's when she and Barry became so tight."

"Tight? Really?"

"Sure. Not only are they good friends, but from what I understand, the Shuberts own about twenty-five percent of the bank's stock, to the Redmond family's fifty-one."

Brash pulled into *Tasty's* parking lot and finagled his big truck into the drive-through ordering lane. Madison waited until he had ordered their coffee before she said excitedly, "You know what this means, don't you?"

"That if we show them your phone app, you're one step closer to a free drink?"

"No, silly!" On second thought, she handed him her cell phone. "Well, okay, that too. But I'm talking about tying Barry Redmond and Molly Shubert to the Christmas Crimes!"

"Who mentioned the Christmas Crimes? I'm trying to tie him to the drug and gambling ring."

"But you suspect it's all mixed up together, so it's sort of the same thing. Until my enlightening conversation with Granny Bert, I would never have suspected Mrs. Shubert of something like this, but you should hear the things she did!" Her eyes glowed with excitement, knowing she was onto something. She ticked off the points, one by one. "Befriended a woman who took ill and suddenly died of a drug overdose. Drugs Molly Shubert had access to, by the way. Alienated the woman's children and ingratiated herself, instead. Planned a trip to Tahiti, supposedly for the poor woman, which she quickly turned into her own honeymoon with the grieving widower. Gave up her baby for her sister to raise, so that she could pick up a romance with a Redmond, the Redmond she *thought* would inherit the bank. Dumped him and married the pharmacist, a man not only old enough to be her father but one who owned stock in that very bank." Running out of fingers as well as breath, she paused to see Brash's reaction and to drag in a deep breath of air.

"Wait a minute. Are you seriously accusing Molly Shubert of the first Mrs. Shubert's death?"

"I don't know. Maybe. It certainly seems suspicious, don't you think?"

The experienced lawman remained neutral, unswayed by her enthusiastic rant. "I don't have enough details to form an opinion."

"Okay, fair enough. But there is definitely a connection here, just as I suspected. Did you know that Molly Shubert is Danielle Applegate's biological mother? She and Charmaine are sisters."

"No, actually, I didn't."

"See!" she cried triumphantly.

"Not really. So, Molly lets her sister raise her child. That doesn't prove she killed anyone, or that she orchestrated an elaborate scheme to steal people's Christmas gifts. And it certainly doesn't implicate Barry Redmond. I'm sorry, sweetheart, but that's not enough to build a case."

"There's more. This ties Molly to Danielle, Danielle to Tom Haskell, and now Molly to Barry Redmond. You already know about Tom Haskell's ties to the gambling ring. It's all connected."

"Maybe so," Brash said, rolling up to the window, "but no DA in the world would take on this case with nothing more than that to go on."

"Hello!" the cashier chirped, sliding the window glass open.

Recognition dawned upon them at the same time.

Brash realized it was the young woman from the stalled vehicle. Under the bright lights, he easily detected vivid streaks of pink running through her shoulder-length brown hair.

Judging by the frightened look in her eyes, she recognized him as the man her accomplice had robbed.

Neither could acknowledge their previous encounter without implicating themselves.

She stuttered out the amount due and Brash silently handed it over. The nametag on her uniform said 'Jaclyn.'

"Hi, Jaclyn," he said stiffly. "Worked here long?"

"Just started," she claimed.

Madison leaned over and peered at the cashier. Despite her frustration at being interrupted in the middle of her argument, and at Brash for not seeing her point, she managed a smile for the young woman. "I know you've been here at least a few weeks. You were working the night my daughter and I came through. You commented on how we managed to get a—" Madison stopped in the middle of her sentence. Her eyes widened as it all began to make sense. She stumbled awkwardly through the rest of her sentence. "—a big box in my car."

Trying to hide her nervousness, Madison took a large gulp from the cup Brash handed her and promptly scalded her tongue. She spewed out the offending liquid, making quite the mess.

"Sweetheart, are you okay?" Brash worried. When he asked for napkins, the attendant threw a handful at him before snapping her window closed.

Rolling the truck forward, Brash focused more on Madison than the girl's rude dismissal. "Are you sure you're all right?"

Still coughing and sputtering, Madison nodded as she wiped up her mess. "I had it all wrong," she lamented. "Go ahead. Go ahead and say I told you so."

"What are you talking about?"

"You said to always question coincidence. Find the link, no matter how small. But I took it too far. I was too focused on the jewelry store, and the links I thought I found between all the different people. I was so busy trying to make that theory work, I completely missed the most obvious link of all!"

"I think that hot coffee burned off a few brain cells," Brash muttered. "What link are you talking about?"

Madison waved a stained napkin in the air, flashing the *Tasty's* logo. "The drive-through! That's how they're doing it! This is the common link."

"The drive-through window," Brash thoughtfully murmured, trying the idea on for size. "They can see inside every vehicle that pulls up."

"Exactly! And all the victims, including myself, stopped here on our way out of town, our cars loaded down like flashing neon signs, practically begging someone to rob us!" She flounced back against the seat, everything so much clearer in hindsight. "Vanessa, Mitzi, and Marilyn all specifically mentioned stopping at *Tasty's,* but I didn't make the connection. And now, seeing the napkin, I remember seeing these exact ones at the Carrs' house and in the photos of Tom Berlin's vehicle. This has to be the link!"

Already out on the road again, Brash's foot faltered on the gas pedal. He needed proof before charging in and making an arrest. Besides, he had no jurisdiction in Brazos County.

Despite her sputtered protest, he continued toward home. "Let's talk this out, babe," he reasoned. "So, you're saying a drive-through attendant—like Jaclyn back there—sees the cars loaded down, somehow alerts an accomplice, and then the accomplice follows the victims back to their homes and robs them?"

"Something like that, yes. Or stops them along the roadside, whichever the case may be."

His mind raced ahead. Jaclyn hadn't been at the window the night the ring was stolen, but she *had* been wearing a uniform. The older cashier on duty had all but smirked at his love-addled brain. That could explain why he didn't recall seeing Jaclyn. She could have been in the background, watching him gaze at the velvet box while visions of romance danced in his head. He tried now to remember if a car had gone around him that night along the road. She would have needed to be ahead of him, he realized, to conveniently stall in the middle of the highway.

"We'd need to see schedules," he thought aloud. "See who was working on each occasion. Unless there's more than one person involved,"—he could place the pink-haired Jaclyn there on at least two occurrences—"we would have to place our suspect on duty during every single shopping excursion."

"Jaclyn was definitely working the night we were there. I remember Bethani spoke to her and I asked if she knew her."

"Did she?"

"No, but she thought she looked familiar, and someone said their cousin worked there. Bethani thought that might be her."

"Do you remember if that person was Addison Bishop?"

"Come to think of it, I believe it was." She looked over at him, clearly impressed. "How did you know that? Do you know that girl Jaclyn?"

"I've seen her before." The vague acknowledgment was all he would admit to. "I vaguely remember that Connie Bishop and Luis Gonzales had a daughter who would be about the same age as this girl, which would make her a cousin to Addison. She used to go by Jackie, but I think it's the same girl. She had a bad habit of hanging with the wrong crowd, which included Fowler and a couple of other troublemakers."

Warming to the theory, Brash continued, "But things are beginning to make sense. Word is that Dickey Fowler's girlfriend has an important job somewhere around here. I assumed 'important' referred to her pay grade, but maybe they were talking about a completely different kind of payoff. If this is their gig, the nice Christmas he kept bragging about will be at their victims' expense."

"'Important' must have meant important to their theft ring!"

"Exactly. It's a pretty sweet set-up, when you think about it. If she sees a car loaded down and recognizes someone from her hometown, all she has to do is tell Fowler. He knows where everyone lives and can case the houses before breaking in."

"That explains why no other towns have been hit, but what about the car jackings?"

"Maybe she saw the episode where they installed your hi-tech alarm and knew breaking into the Big House wasn't an option. Maybe your packed car was too good of a deal to pass up. It might have been worth the risk of robbing you alongside the road. Same with Ted Berlin, who wasn't from The Sisters, but who had at least two flat-screen televisions, clearly visible, in the back of his truck."

"That is so low, stealing people's Christmas presents like that!"

"If you don't mind, I need to call the station."

"Go ahead. I'll see what I can find out about Jaclyn." Seeing his puzzled expression, she held up her phone. "Social media. If that doesn't yield results, I'll call Granny."

By the time Brash hung up from his call, Madison wore a sly smile upon her face. "Bingo! Jaclyn Suzanne Gonzales, twenty-one years old, graduated from The Sisters High. Works at *Tasty's* and is in a relationship with Dickey Fowler. Goes by the nicknames Jackie and J'Bad. Has aspirations of moving to Austin and becoming a true barista, or trying out for the cast of *Big Brother.*"

"You got all that from social media?"

"Would you like to know what she had for lunch? She posted a picture on InstaGram."

"What is wrong with people these days?" Brash grumbled.

"Nothing better to do, I guess," she shrugged. She looked down at her phone, hovering over the *Tasty's* app. "You know,

I still can't believe I missed this. Most of the victims talked about *Tasty's* and how they liked to stop by on their way out of town. I can't believe I was so hung up on the jewelry store angle that I didn't even see this one."

"Hey, I missed it, too. Don't beat yourself up over it. And to be honest, I'm not sure you're wrong about—"

"Uh, Brash," Madison interrupted in a nervous tone. "What are those flashing lights ahead? And why is that car coming up behind us so fast?"

"I'm not sure." His voice was a bit too tight for her comfort. He put both hands on the wheel and alternated his attention between the front window and the rear-view mirror. "Let me guess. That *Tasty's* app has access to your microphone, right?"

"I—I don't know, why?" She glanced down at her phone and pulled up the app's details.

"Those aren't regulation lights. The color pattern is off. And whoever this is behind us is making no attempt to go around."

"Okay, yes, the microphone was accessed, but—"

"But that's another trick they have up their sleeves. Just like that *TossUp* app, when people pull up to the drive-through, they can access their microphones and listen in to private conversations. People might talk about what they bought, even where they're going to hide the presents until Christmas Day."

Brash kept his speed steady, even though they were quickly approaching the vehicle sitting in the middle of the road, emergency lights flashing. "Which means they know we're onto them. Delete the app from your phone. Now."

Her hands shook as she did as told. He dialed his own phone and barked off orders. Forced to slow his speed, Brash instructed her to open the glove compartment. "There's a small gun inside. Get it out and slip it into my boot."

With clumsy fingers, Madison retrieved the tiniest pistol she had ever seen. "It looks like a toy."

"It's a .380. Slip it inside my boot and under my sock. Pull my pants leg back down."

"Wh—What's going on, Brash?" She didn't have to say she was frightened; the tremor in her voice said it for her.

"I think the Christmas Crimes have been nothing more than a ploy, a distraction to pull our attention away from the drug and gambling ring. I think we were onto something earlier, and they heard us. It's starting to make sense now, to pull together into one big web."

"What web? What sense?"

"Just follow my lead, sweetheart. It's going to be okay. I love you."

"I—I love you, too, but why do you feel the need to tell me that at this particular moment?" Her voice rose with panic as they were forced to slow down even more.

"It's always a good time to tell you I love you, sweetheart." The words would have been more convincing if he had looked at her as he spoke. Instead, his eyes were peeled on the man stepping from the stopped vehicle. In the dark night, the flashing lights were blinding, but he immediately detected the crumpled game warden's uniform and the wrong-style hat upon Dickey Fowler's head.

"Not again!" Madison wailed. "And in almost the exact same place!"

"Hold on, sweetheart, this might get rough," Brash warned, "because we're not stopping!"

He jerked the steering wheel to the right and gunned the engine, plunging his truck off the shoulder of the road, through the bar ditch, and fishtailing his way back toward the pavement. Madison hung on for dear life, feeling like a rag doll in a dog's mouth. The seatbelt bit into her chest and her head banged against the side window glass. She bit back a scream as the truck lunged up and over the rim of pavement. Just for a moment, they were airborne. The tires slammed back onto asphalt and her stomach turned over.

"You okay?" Brash yelled, fighting for control of the powerful vehicle.

"Y—Yes!"

"It's not over yet." His voice was deceptively calm, but she knew he was worried. He glanced in the mirror. "They're coming after us."

"Can't we go any faster?"

"It's a curvy road and a dark night, but I'm going as fast as I can." He pressed the gas pedal down as far as he dared.

"I think we're losing them," Madison said, turning in her seat to look out the back window. "I'll call Cutter." She wheeled back around as she spoke. "He'll—Brash! Watch out!"

Almost invisible against the dark pavement, a huge black feral hog and five baby piglets trotted across the road. The truck was tall enough to skim over the piglets, but Brash knew the sow was big enough, and solid enough, to do major damage. He jerked the wheel and felt the truck go into a skid. The mother hog chose that moment to bolt, running straight into the path of the spinning truck.

The seatbelts locked and the airbags inflated, as the truck came to a sharp and abrupt halt.

18

"Are you all right?" Brash demanded.

"I—I think so. You?"

"Yeah." He sounded more disgusted than hurt. He swore quietly, a habit he was trying hard to break.

"I think this situation warrants strong words," she commiserated. She waved at the dark particles that choked the air around them. "Is this... this isn't smoke, is it?" Her voice rose in alarm.

"No, it's from the airbags," he assured her. "Can you get out of your seatbelt?"

"I think so. If my fingers will work."

"We need to get out of here."

The words had barely left his lips when both front doors jerked open. Two men stood on either side of the truck. One wore a long, shaggy beard and a limp game warden uniform. The other three wore Santa suits, complete with snowy white beards and mustaches.

"You two have been mighty naughty this year," one of the Santas sneered. He was so skinny the black belt circled twice around his waist, in a desperate attempt to keep his red flocked pants from falling down. If not for the gun in his hand, the situation might have been comical.

"So have you, Havlicek," Brash drawled.

The scrawny Santa stepped back in surprise, unprepared for the possibility of being recognized. "Get out!" he spat, motioning with his gun.

Brash tried to reason with them. "Don't do something we'll all regret. If you boys will just back off, you can get back in your vehicles and drive away. I won't even write up a report."

Bernie was having none of it. "You're just full of Christmas wishes, now ain't cha?"

"He's full of something!" Dickey Fowler giggled. His eyes were too bright, their glassy sheen a dead giveaway to his condition. The man was higher than a kite.

Brash studied the other men, trying to determine their identities behind the fake beards. He thought one was Bernie's younger brother Doug, but he couldn't see the fourth man well. He stood behind Bernie, half-hidden in shadow. That, alone, raised Brash's suspicion.

"Don't make me repeat myself. I said get out of the truck."

Brash reached for Maddy's hand. "She's getting out on my side," he said, his voice brooking no argument. It meant she would have to crawl over the center console, but he wasn't letting her away from his side, gun or no gun.

"Leave your phones," Bernie called.

"Mine's wedged in the dash." Maddy tossed the words over her shoulder as she scrambled toward Brash.

Bernie tried to retrieve the turquoise case from between the dashboard and windshield, but it refused to budge. "Well, dang, that sucker is stuffed in there tight," he muttered. He gave up after one more try. "Just as well. Won't be needing it no more."

"And yours, Chief?" Santa Doug asked, holding his hand out to receive it as Brash slid from the seat. Despite his best efforts, the man shrank back as the policeman loomed over him. The Havliceks were of slight build and wiry muscle.

"No idea," Brash shrugged. "Lost it when we went into a skid."

"Then find it."

Seeing the message in his eyes, Madison waited in the driver's seat while Brash bent to look for his phone. She shifted her legs so that the men on the other side of the truck had an obstructed view of his search. He fumbled around for a few minutes, his efforts exaggerated. Madison had no idea what he was doing, but she suspected he was up to something.

"Hand over the damn phone!" Doug said, growing impatient.

Brash turned to glare at the man, matching him tone for tone. "I would, if I could find it. Bernie, see if it slid over that way. Things were rolling every which way during that wild ride."

While Bernie searched under the passenger seat and through bags and debris thrown against the floorboards, Madison felt something slip into the top of her ankle boot. It was all she could do not to jump from the sensation of cold metal against her skin. Something vibrated under the seat, but Brash's hooded expression warned her not to react.

"Oh, here it is," Brash said abruptly. He tossed the device upward toward Dickey, whose reflexes were dulled by the drugs. He grabbed for the phone and managed to juggle it for several seconds. When Doug decided to snatch it from his partner's bumbling hands, Brash whisked the gun away from his own inept hold.

"Not so fast," the fourth Santa said, his voice so unnaturally low it could only be a disguise. He had silently moved from one side of the truck to the other. Still mostly hidden in shadow, but Brash had no problem detecting the high-powered rifle in his hands. "Give the gun back to Santa."

"Here. Doug." Brash shoved the gun into the man's hands, daring him to deny his identity. Satisfied with the answering tremor he saw in the man's hands, Brash leaned back and asked, almost casually, "So what now, Doug? Where do you and Bernie plan on taking us? Please tell me Dickey won't be driving. Or your other Santa pal, there, the one with the Browning 25-06. Nice gun, by the way. Fancy stock. What is that, maple?"

"Shut up. What do you think this is, a tailgate party?" Bernie screamed. He slammed the door so hard the glass rattled in its frame. A small squeak escaped from Madison, calling their attention to the fact that she still sat inside the vehicle.

"I see Her Highness is still on her throne," the unidentified Santa snarked. This time, he forgot to lower his voice.

Madison sucked in a sharp breath. She made a subtle move toward Brash, as much to alert him as to draw comfort from his nearness. The reference couldn't be a coincidence. This had to be the same man who was in the cave, the one that gave orders to dispose of her and Derron. The big boss.

"How are things up at the North Pole, Santa?" Brash asked in a lazy tone. Madison jerked her gaze to her boyfriend, wondering what he was up to. He obviously had a plan of some sort, if only a plan to throw them off their game with his amiable attitude.

He gave a one-word reply, hardly what Brash was hoping for. "Cold."

"And the reindeer?"

His voice low and hard, the Santa with the rifle nudged it in Doug's direction. "Santa, maybe you should remind our friend this isn't that tailgate party, after all. He seems to be confused."

When Doug would have punched Brash in the stomach, the more agile officer easily deflected the move. He actually grinned at the slower man. "What are you talking about? This isn't a party? Three men in Santa suits and one in a game warden uniform stop us in the middle of the Bryan highway, and you're telling me this isn't a party? Dickey, here, seems to be having a party of his own, judging by that stupid grin on his face."

"I don't know what you're up to," Bernie said, "but knock it off! Get in the car, both of you." He jerked Madison's arm to pull her from the truck, his manner rough.

Without warning, Brash issued a harsh blow to Bernie's mid-section, doubling the man over. Like lightning, he turned his fists to Dickey. One punch sent the younger man sprawled out on the ground. Brash had Doug in a chokehold and the pistol within his grasp when the long report of a rifle rent the still night air.

"The next bullet won't go high," the angry fourth Santa ground out. "Now everyone get in the car and get out of here. Move!"

Lurching into action, the other three men scrambled to follow orders. Brash helped Madison from the truck, whispering a brief, "Trust me, babe. We'll get out of this." He allowed

Bernie to lead them to the waiting car, where the skinny Santa unceremoniously shoved them inside and then crawled in after them, shutting the door. Dickey squeezed in on the other side. Doug got behind the wheel, while the fourth Santa took his own vehicle. He shrewdly traveled behind them, his lights on bright to keep Brash from identifying his ride.

They turned down the first dirt road they came to, a county road that led to the back side of Riverton. Hearing sirens in the distance, Brash looked into the rear-view mirror and saw that the reinforcements he called for were just a few minutes late in arriving. Two patrol cars and Cutter's personal truck sailed down the highway past them, lights and sirens at full blast.

"What the heck is that about?" Doug asked. He glared at Brash through his rearview mirror. "How'd you do it? How'd you get a message to them?"

"I don't know what you're talking about," Brash lied. "I guess someone came across my truck in the middle of the road and called 9-1-1."

"Boys, put the blindfolds on 'em," Doug instructed. "And tie their hands."

"Is that really necessary?" Brash asked tediously. "We've cooperated with you so far. Doesn't that count for something?"

"You punched me in the gut!" Bernie complained.

"My jaw still hurts," Dickey said, but the goofy smile remained on his face.

"So does my throat." Doug cleared it now, for good measure. "And it's blindfolds or we knock you over the head. Your choice."

"Blindfold, please," Madison was quick to say.

Bernie pulled a rag from the pocket of his baggy Santa pants and put it over her eyes. As he tied a knot in the back, she pulled away. "Hey, the hair. Leave some, please."

"Yes, Your Highness," he sneered.

"Now you sound like Barry Redmond," she muttered.

Beside her, Bernie went perfectly still. And in that moment, Madison knew who the big boss was.

Stunned, she turned her head to Brash, but of course she could not see him. She groped for his hand and squeezed it tightly, hoping to convey her deep concern for their safety.

He squeezed back, just as tightly.

After a series of turns and curves and miles of travel, Brash became hopelessly disoriented. He did rather well the first several miles, guessing the roads they turned down and anticipating their next move. But after a while, he lost count in his head. He could no longer judge distance between one turn and the next. Some roads seemed unfamiliar. At one point, Doug pulled into an apparent driveway, backed out, and made a circle. By the time they started forward again, Brash wasn't sure of the direction they traveled. He finally gave up and tried to relax.

Back at the truck, he had tried stalling as long as he could. He turned on the police-band radio beneath his seat, setting the dial to one-way transmit. He tried to give dispatch as many details as he could, including the identity of his captors. Unable to clearly identify the fourth man, he at least gave details about his weapon. That was a sweet rifle he had, most likely custom made. Maybe someone would recognize the description and know who owned it.

If only they had arrived two minutes earlier, he and Maddy might not be sitting here blindfolded, squished between two idiots. If not for the car behind them, Brash would have made a move for the door, long ago. He had no doubt he and Maddy could have gotten away from the not-so-bright trio, and handily so. He also had no doubt that the fourth Santa would have no problem in shooting either one of them, should they attempt an escape. So here he sat, his hands bound and his eyes covered, feeling uncharacteristically useless. It wasn't a feeling he often experienced, and certainly not one he welcomed.

"Come on, Doug, don't you think it's time you took us home?" He tried reasoning with the Santa behind the wheel. "Now you're adding kidnapping to the list of charges against you. Don't you want to be around to see your kids graduate from high school? Because kidnapping carries a stiff prison sentence."

"There won't be any kidnapping charges, you dimwit," Bernie claimed. "Ignore him, Doug. He's just trying to yank your chain."

"They don't use ball and chains in prison anymore," Brash said, his tone conversational. "They use ankle monitors. Magnetic, so they can shut you down with a touch of a button. Can't lift your feet, even if you're standing in the middle of an angry prison riot, getting beat to a pulp."

He could sense Doug's nervousness. His foot faltered on the gas pedal, causing the car to slow down. Behind them, the rifle-toting Santa tapped on his horn. Doug sped up, but his driving skills suffered. He took turns more sharply. Hit more potholes. Scraped against overhanging tree limbs.

From the backseat, his brother spewed out a string of curse words, followed by, "Don't let him get to you, Doug! He's full of bull. I'm telling you, there won't be no kidnapping charges."

"Murder charges carry a life sentence," Brash reminded them. He squeezed Madison's hand as he spoke in a low, solemn voice, hoping she had fallen asleep. She no longer squirmed beside him, resting against his arm in what he hoped was slumber.

"Who—Who said anything about murder?" Bernie squeaked.

Brash heard the warble in his voice, caught the scent of fear upon the air. Bernie had orders to kill them both.

For the first time tonight, Brash worried they might be in actual danger.

19

When the car finally stopped, Brash gently nudged Madison to rouse her. On his other side, Dickey softly snored.

Bernie pushed the car door open and crawled out. "What are you waitin' on?" he grumbled with impatience. "Get out."

Stiff from sitting in a cramped position for so long, and sore from their rough ride earlier in the truck, Brash knew it was hard for Maddy to follow the abrupt command. He murmured encouragement as she eased off the seat, which allowed him more room to unfold his own large body within the cramped confines. With Dickey still sleeping against the door, he slid the length of the seat and exited on her side. His knee popped when he straightened his legs and stood.

"Getting old?" Bernie goaded him.

"Happens when a man works for a living," Brash replied evenly.

"Work, hell! You played for a living. Wish I got paid for playing a football game, and for telling other folks how to do it. You always did have it too easy."

Brash made no comment. He was listening for clues on their location. Judging from the near silence, he guessed they were well outside of town. He heard no cars, no televisions, no telltale rustle of life. Then again, it was nighttime. Probably around midnight, he would imagine. A sense of timing was another thing he lost during their wandering drive.

"You just going to stand there?" Doug asked. "Get inside the house."

"Didn't know we were at a house," Brash said. "Can't see a thing, remember?"

It was a lie. Lucky for him, Dickey was either too high or too inept to tie a proper blindfold. Most likely both, Brash imagined, but all the better for him. The cloth band over his eyes wasn't only slightly crooked, but the fool had put the thickest part on his forehead, allowing sensation of light to filter through the thinner material covering his eyes. He could actually see his feet, but when Bernie pushed him forward and told him to walk, he pretended to stumble over a clot of dirt.

"Armadillo holes," Bernie snickered. "Don't break an ankle."

"Where's Dickey?" Doug barked, noticing they were short a man.

"He fell asleep not long after the sharp 'S' curve on Sawyer Road," Brash said. He wanted to rattle them, let them know he was paying attention. He heard Doug curse and stomp his way around the car, where he jerked the backdoor open.

From the sounds of it, Dickey fell out in an undignified heap.

The bumbling trio led their captives across a yard littered with holes, weeds, and assorted trash. Brash got a whiff of an offensive odor. A familiar buzzing noise confirmed his suspicions, particularly loud in the still night. They were at the Fowler shack, now minus the barking dog.

One of the men went first and opened the door. No one bothered to warn their captives of steps, but before Madison stumbled into them, Brash cautioned her.

"Can you see out of that blindfold?" Bernie asked suspiciously.

"No, I don't need to." Brash denied. "Y'all stomp around like horses. A deaf man could hear your boots on those wooden steps."

He didn't know if Bernie believed him or not. Just in case, he lifted his foot too early and stumbled forward. Being banged in the shin was worth earning their laughter and, he hoped, their trust.

"We'll tie them to those chairs," Bernie decided. "Dickey, put two of them back to back." After a series of bumps and scrapes as Dickey tried to follow directions, Bernie cursed in exasperation. "Not that way, you fool! Put the backs together."

Best Brash could tell, the fourth Santa hadn't followed them to the house. He heard no engine behind them when they first pulled up, no rustle of footsteps in the background, no sighs of frustration over his inept cohorts. Of the four of them, the unidentified man was clearly the smartest of them all, which made him the most dangerous.

"What happened to your rifle-toting buddy?" Brash asked. He allowed them to push him down into one of the chairs, noting the way the legs groaned beneath his weight. With any luck, the strain would be too much and he could use the busted frame to saw away the binds they were sure to tie around them.

"Never you mind about him," Doug advised. "You have enough worries of your own."

"So, what's the plan? What are you going to do with us?"

"Maybe we'll just leave you two lovebirds here a few days," Bernie jeered. "Think of this as your little love nest, just the two of you. Plenty of time for bonding, while the rest of us celebrate Christmas."

"Don't forget that big poker game you have tomorrow night."

At mention of the game, Brash felt the men stiffen around them.

"Hey," Dickey whispered loudly, "how's he know about that?"

"I don't know," Bernie snarled.

"Does he know it's going to be out at the Gonzales' old barn?"

"He does now, you fool."

"What's he going to do about it? He'll be tied up here, with his old lady. At least he don't know we're moving a big shipment of drugs at the same time. Been cooking them right here under his nose, in the pharmacy basement. Best place in the world to hide illegal drugs, right in among the—umph! Hey! Why'd ya punch me in the gut?"

"Shut. Up."

"You don't have to be so testy," Dickey whined.

"Just tie them up. Pull it nice and tight."

Brash pulled slightly away from the back of the chair and puffed his chest, just enough to allow wiggle room after the ropes were tied, but not enough to call attention to the fact. Not that Dickey would ever notice, but the Havlicek brothers weren't quite as stupid as their third cousin was. Not as much inbreeding on their branch of the family tree, he supposed. He still cringed every time he recalled the story behind Dickey Fowler's lineage.

After circling around them three times with a rope, Dickey stood back and bragged about his handiwork.

"Doug, check the knots," Bernie instructed his brother. "Make sure the idiot did it right."

"Hey, I'm tired of you calling me an idiot."

"I'm tired of you acting like one."

Brash bulked up again, as Doug tugged on the rope and made certain the knot would hold. "Not bad," he acknowledged.

"This ain't my first rodeo, you know," the younger man crowed. "You 'member that tobacco shop over in Riverton, the one that got robbed twice, two times in a row? With the clerks tied up in the backroom? That was yours truly. And—"

"And I told you. Shut. Up. He's right there, listening to everything you say!"

"And just for the record," Brash broke in dryly, "twice means two times. You don't have to be redundant."

"Well, thank you for that there English lesson, mister police man," Dickey said in an exaggerated drawl. "And no need to use fancy words we don't understand."

"Can we go home now?" Doug wanted to know. "I promised my old lady I'd help her put up the tree tonight. She's already going to be pissed, without me staying out all night."

"It's not even one o'clock yet."

"Too late to put up a stupid Christmas tree, though."

"Hey," Dickey said, his voice brightening as he came up with an original thought. "Go in the back room yonder and look for something nice to give her. I found some real nice earrings under that schoolteacher's tree. Your old lady might like those."

Brash chided himself for not searching the house more thoroughly the first time he was here. Disgusted by the sheer filth of the place, and angry about the pilfered electricity, he hadn't paid enough attention to the covered piles and the trash bags in either of the side rooms. The loot from the Christmas Crimes was stashed here in this dump, and he had missed it. He owned that mistake.

Doug stomped his way to the other room, complaining about the lack of light.

"Yeah, I lost electricity the other day," Dickey said. "Been meaning to hook it back up, but I'm hardly out here no more."

"This house needs a bulldozer put to it," Bernie said.

"Hey, this is my inheritance." Dickey sounded truly offended by the comment.

Bernie snorted. He gave his brother a few moments to bang around in the other room, then called out to him. "Are you done with your shopping yet? Because we need to get out of here. We have trucks to load."

"That's why the boss man went on ahead. And I'm going home after this." Doug tromped closer, his voice taking on a satisfied ring. "Patty will flip out over these earrings. And she's always wanted one of these fuzzy robes. Just her size, too."

"Extra jumbo?" Dickey snickered.

"Full bodied," Doug corrected, sharp distinction in his voice. "I like to know I'm holding a woman in my arms, not a twig."

Dickey bristled. "Are you calling my woman a twig? Because that sounds like an insult to me."

"Would you two shut up?" Bernie barked.

Ignoring him, the other two men continued to argue, but their voices faded as they stomped from the room. The door slammed behind them, leaving the old house eerily silent. When Brash heard the engine start, he heaved a sigh of relief.

"Are you okay, sweetheart? You haven't said a word."

"I didn't want to call attention to myself," she admitted. "And I was afraid I might say the wrong thing. What was all that about, back at the car? What was that vibration I felt under the seat?"

"I turned on my police radio. I was trying to give them as much information as possible, so they would know who had us and what we were up against."

"If only they had gotten there a few minutes earlier, we wouldn't be in this fix! I take it we're at Dickey Fowler's house?" Her voice revealed her disgust.

"We're at his dump, all right. And apparently, so is all the Christmas loot."

"At least our hands are tied in front of us this time." The single other time she had been tied to a chair, she had been much more uncomfortable, her arms bound behind her. "Can you untie the rope? And what in the devil's name is this smell? This rope reeks."

"I think he used it to tie his dog outside, if that tells you anything."

"Ugh." He felt the shiver in her shoulders. "But I didn't hear a dog, except in the far distance."

"He left it tied with no food. I called it in to animal welfare the first time I was here."

"I wish they had taken this rope with them," Madison bemoaned. "I'm about to gag from the smell."

"Breathe through your mouth as much as you can," Brash suggested. "I have a little wiggle room. I think I can get out of it." He tugged, but nothing happened, prompting him to add, "Eventually."

A moment ticked by, before Madison announced, "I know who the big boss is."

"Barry Redmond."

"Yes! What was your tip off?"

"It just all makes sense now. And even though he kept to the shadows and I never got a good look at his face, I saw his hands. His nails were manicured. Barry is the only man around here I know of who pampers his hands like that. And the fancy gun was a good tip off."

"I thought I recognized his cologne. He always wears way too much, like he swims in the expensive stuff. And when I mentioned his name, Bernie got too nervous. It was a dead giveaway."

"So, you were right all along, sweetheart. They are all tied in this together. Molly, Tom Haskell, Barry. It's hard to know if Danielle is involved, but the others definitely are."

"Why else would Tom Haskell be hanging around the jewelry store, if she wasn't involved?"

"I have a theory about that."

He told her the story Charlie had relayed to him, about the girl Tom Haskell hooked up with from The Sisters and took to Colorado. "Your dad thought her name may have been named Mary, but he wasn't sure. I think it could have been Molly," Brash said. "The timeline is right. We know that Molly left town with some guy she met and came back pregnant. Now Tom gets out of prison, and one of the first places he heads to is the mall, where he hangs out with Danielle, who just happens to be Molly's daughter."

"You think Tom Haskell is her *father?*"

"Makes sense, don't you think?"

"Yeah, I guess it does," Madison agreed, sounding somewhat dazed.

Brash continued to tug against the ropes. "No thanks to Doug's help, Dickey tied these ropes a lot better than he tied my blindfold. Mine is all but falling off. What about yours?"

"Tangled quite snuggly in my hair, I'm afraid. Can't see a thing."

"Can you reach my phone? I put it in your right boot leg."

"What did you throw at Dickey?"

"My burner phone, the one I use undercover."

That gave her pause. "You work undercover? When?"

"I'm a special investigator for the county, remember? Sometimes I go undercover."

"Like half the state of Texas doesn't recognize you!"

"Can't this conversation wait?" he asked impatiently. "Can you reach the phone, or not?"

She tried to bend far enough to reach her leg, but the ropes were too tight. "No, but I can reach mine."

"I thought yours was wedged in my dashboard."

"That was just the case. I took it out of its cover when I spilled coffee all over it. I slipped my phone into my front pocket when no one was watching."

"That's my girl," Brash chuckled.

"Sadly enough, this isn't my first rodeo, either." Her voice was resigned.

"You gotta admit, moving back to The Sisters has added adventure to your life."

"It almost makes me miss the good old days of the staid and boring life I once led."

He sounded concerned. "Really?'

"I said almost."

While both worked against the bindings of their hands—Brash to loosen the ropes and Maddy to retrieve the phone in her pocket—they fell silent. A few grunts punctuated the dark stillness of the room. Their frustration mounted with each failed attempt, but neither gave up. Failure wasn't an option.

After a while, Madison paused her efforts long enough to rest her strained muscles. She pulled in a few deep breaths of air, reeking rope and all.

"Brash? There's something I want to tell you."

He didn't respond immediately, concentrating on freeing his hands. If he could break the duct tape on his wrists, he might be able to twist one arm behind him and untie the knot on the rope... Grunting with the effort, he finally said, "What is it, sweetheart?"

"First, I want to say I love you. Truly and deeply. More than I've ever loved anyone in my life. Other than my children, of course, but that's different."

"Of course. And I love you the same way, Maddy." His voice was deep and rich, filled with sincerity as he said, "This is forever love."

He felt her pull in a deep breath of air. Tilting her head back to touch his, she spoke in the darkness. "You've asked me before about my marriage to Gray, but I wasn't ready to tell you the whole story. I am now."

Brash interrupted her before she could go any further. "Hold on. I'm more than willing to listen to whatever you have to say, but only if you would have told me this anyway. *Not* because we're tied up here in an abandoned house and you think we won't make it out." His voice turned to steel. "Because we will make it out, sweetheart. My team is out searching for us. They've called in reinforcements by now, and they're combing the countryside for us, as well as for those sorry souls who brought us here. So, this isn't the end. Far from it." His voice softened again. "But if you still want to talk, I want to listen."

"I do. I should have told you this a long time ago, but I've been trying so hard to keep my kids from knowing the sordid details of those last couple of years. I know they probably suspect, but *thinking* something and *knowing* it are two different things. All they have left of their father are their memories, and I just don't want to destroy those for them."

"You're a wonderful mother, Maddy." His voice was rich with emotion.

"I try. And I tried to be a good wife. And I *was*, at first, I think. Just like Gray started out as a good husband. We had some good years together. Happy years. But then… things started to change. Life became so complicated…"

Madison released a shaky breath, carefully tiptoeing into memories of the past.

"It started when Gray branched off on his own, starting up an investment company. His parents helped fund it, of course. I've already told you how they pushed us to buy a bigger house in a better neighborhood. Never mind if we couldn't afford it. It was the same with the business. If we looked successful, we would be successful. To them, it was all about appearances, and they hounded that mentality into Gray's mind. We had to have an extravagant office in Dallas' most exclusive office building, had to entertain clients at the best restaurants in the city. It was all about show. All smoke and mirrors.

"I worried about the expenses, but Gray said I should leave the details to him. He claimed I had enough to worry over, what with the kids' schedules and entertaining friends and clients several times a week. I worked with him at the office, but it was hard to juggle it all. Annette insisted we needed to hire help. I refused to hire a nanny, but I finally caved on hiring a receptionist. And just like that, Gwendolyn stepped into our lives."

It still hurt to say her name, but Madison swallowed hard and powered through.

"I have to admit, at first I thought she was a godsend. Having help at the office made life so much easier. I even let her plan our social calendar, something I had little interest in doing. It was great. All I had to do was find a sitter, put on a pretty dress, and show up with a smile. But then one night, Bethani was running a fever, and I couldn't go with Gray to a business dinner. Would I mind terribly if he took Gwendolyn in my stead, he asked."

She pulled in another deep breath and slowly released it. "That's how it started. That's how Gwendolyn began to take over. And I let her, because it made my life easier. And Gray let her, because... well, because he always took the easy way out. Why didn't she join us at the Honeycutt dinner, he suggested. She was so good with clients. Young and attractive, and such a good conversationalist. Maybe she should go with us to the Chicago convention, he said. And if I'd rather do some shopping or go sightseeing, rather than sitting in on the meeting with the Tokyo clients, well, Gwendolyn spoke limited Japanese. She could fill in for me.

"That became the new mantra in our house. I should go to Blake's baseball game. Gwendolyn would fill in for me at the business dinner." Madison acted out the parts, surprising herself when her words came out more animated than emotional. "Bethani had a recital? No problem. Gray would just ask Gwendolyn to take my place at the cocktail party. He knew how much I hated those things, after all, and I'd have a much better time at the recital. And don't wait up on him tomorrow night. He and Gwendolyn had to go over a presentation. And about next weekend. We would have to cancel that hiking trip with the Petersons. What? The kids would be crushed? Well, why didn't I go on ahead, and he would stay behind and work on the project. Gwendolyn could fill in for me, and we'd all come out winners in the end."

"Everything but your marriage," Brash noted dryly.

"By then, I'm not sure we even still had a marriage. Oh, we put on a show for the kids. Our friends knew there was something wrong, but once in a blue moon, we'd go out with another couple and pretend we still remembered how to talk to one another. I even quit going into the office, which turned out to be a monumental mistake on my part. Gwendolyn, as you might guess, was excellent at spending money. Our money, anyway. She just loved the concept of spending money to make money, or looking successful to be successful. Gray even gave her a *spending account,* of all things. In hindsight, I suppose it's not uncommon to set your mistress up with some sort of compensation, but it came directly out of our business account, which was already suffering enough on its own.

Hemorrhaging might be the better word. By the time I realized how bad things were, it was too late."

"I'm sorry, sweetheart."

"You can imagine my surprise when I found out that Gray had taken out a second mortgage on our house. Care to gander what he spent the money on?"

"Keeping the business afloat?"

"Oh, no. He used our client's money for that, which is a completely different topic altogether. With *our* money, including most of the money we had set aside to send the twins to college, he bought Gwendolyn a cozy little condo. Guess where that condo was? Five streets over, so he could easily split his time between houses. No need to spend all his time driving, when he could eat an occasional dinner with his wife and kids, slip out to see his girlfriend, and be back in time for breakfast the next morning. He usually just jogged over there, not even bothering with taking a car."

"You didn't know?"

"No." Her voice filled with shame. "I know it makes me look stupid. Looking back, I don't know how I could have missed it. The neighbors had to have known. I mean, come on, five streets. And thankfully, the kids didn't know, either. They didn't know Gwendolyn was more than just Gray's secretary. They didn't know their entire financial security had been squandered five streets over, on a little love nest for their father's mistress. They didn't know their father didn't really have insomnia. That, by the way, was his lame excuse for sleeping in the guest room and for going out on his late-night runs."

Her matter-of-fact delivery began to crack when she relived her children's grief. "But then Gray died in a car wreck, and their world shattered around them. The least I could do was keep up the illusion. They didn't need to know the sordid details. They didn't need to know why she was in the car with him, or why we were losing the house, or why—why we had no savings, no big life insurance policy to fall back on."

"Sweetheart, you weren't stupid," Brash assured her, his deep voice rich with love and admiration. "And while I would love to sit here and talk to you more about what a brave and courageous woman you are for protecting your children that way, and about why I love and admire you so very, very much, I think it's time we get out of here. So if you don't mind, let's save the rest of this discussion for another time."

"Good call," Madison said with a nervous laugh. "And I think I can reach my phone now. The trouble is, I can't see to use it."

"Then allow me," said a cold voice from across the room.

20

T heir heads jerked in the direction of the man's voice, even though their eyes were still bound by the blindfolds. Neither had heard Barry Redmond step into the room.

Brash cursed his own stupidity. He had been so caught up in Madison's heartbreaking story, he hadn't even heard the car approach. Love would be the death of him yet.

"What a touching tale you weave, Your Highness," Barry said, still trying to disguise his voice. "If it's any consolation, your children will never have to know the truth. I promise, your secret will die with you."

"That's very generous of you," Madison said with heavy sarcasm. "I never knew you to have a soft spot. *Barry.*"

She wished she could see his face just then. Knowing his monumental arrogance, he probably thought his identity was a well-guarded secret.

There was a moment of silence while the banker digested the fact that he was no longer incognito. Brash used the time to finish off the ties that once confined his hands. The ropes, however, were still snugly knotted, binding them both to the chairs and rendering him useless.

"So. How did you figure it out?" he finally asked. Giving up the farce altogether, he spoke in his own voice, thereby acknowledging his identity.

Madison waited for Brash to say something, but she could feel him making discreet moves behind her, still trying to work himself free. When he gently nudged her, she understood the message. He wanted her to do the talking, deflecting Barry's attention away from him and therefore buying them more time.

"There were a lot of little things. Your cologne, for one." She couldn't help but goad the banker, imagining the entertaining shade of purple he was sure to turn. "I know you have a lot of stank to cover up, but you really should go lighter on the cologne, Barry. It's a bit overpowering." She went so far as to sniff the air. "On the up side, it does manage to mask the reek of this rope, so for once, I actually approve of your heavy hand."

Behind her, she felt Brash's chuckle, more than heard it.

Unamused, Barry barked out, "What else?"

"I connected the dots. Living in the city for so long, this is one of the things I forgot about small towns. Everyone is connected to everyone else, in one way or another. Take your cohort in crime, for instance, Molly Shubert. And yes, we know about Molly. She was once married to your cousin Randy, so apparently you two go way back. I hear you're not only friends, but that she and her current husband own a substantial interest in your bank. She probably enjoys a bigger slice of the pie with Mr. Shubert than she would have with Randy, but that's beside the point it. The point is, that makes you two business partners, in more ways than one. The bank is the legal connection. The drugs and gambling are the illegal connections."

"Sounds like you think you have it all figured out."

"There's still a few unconnected dots here and there, but it's coming together," Madison said, sounding more confident than she felt. When Brash rubbed his head against hers, she first thought it was a warning. Then she remembered how loose he said his blindfold was. Most likely, he was using the traction to work it loose. Another gentle nudge of his shoulder encouraged her to continue talking.

"I know Molly's daughter was once married to Doug Havlicek. What I don't know is whether that daughter is Randy's child, but until I can connect those dots, let's assume she is. That gives you a nice family connection to the Havlicek clan. We know you have a business connection to them through the drugs. And if I'm not mistaken, my guess is you also have a hand in the hotshot business they run. It makes a nice cover for delivering drugs, doesn't it? With the oil industry hurting the way it is, I wondered how a business like that managed to stay afloat, until I remembered something my mother mentioned earlier. Gosh, was that just today? Or yesterday, I guess it is now. Anyway, she said my father did a couple of runs for them that made him very uncomfortable. You knew my father once worked for them, right?"

"Yes, and I love it. A high and mighty Cessna, working for the Havliceks, of all people!" The touch of mania in his crowing laughter sent an ominous ripple of fear down Madison's spine. She instinctively leaned into Brash for strength.

"Those runs were with your friend Tom Haskell. Dad suspected they were delivering something illegal, so he quit his job after that. My father may be flighty, but for the most part, he's a fairly stand-up guy. At any rate, that got me to connecting more dots. Illegal deliveries, Tom Haskell, gambling ring. Tom is the one who handles the gambling side of your operation, right? He even managed to do so from prison, which I understand is hard to do unless you can afford to bribe a lot of guards. You need a solid backer for that. Someone like a banker, for instance. And of course, he's connected to Molly from way back. I think they may even share a daughter together, Danielle Applegate. Is she part of this, too? That's another dot I haven't fully connected yet, but I'm working on it. How am I doing so far?"

"I think you're dotty."

Behind her, Madison felt Brash shift. If he felt it safe to move, he must know the room was still dark. She wondered if he were reaching for the gun tucked inside his boot. She kept talking, stalling for more time.

Even though Barry couldn't see her in the darkness, she shrugged the best she could while confined by the ropes. That's when she noticed how loose they had become. She faltered out of sheer relief, before remembering not to tip their hand. "Uh... you've called me worse. In fact, that was probably the biggest tip-off of all. That time in the cave, you called me Your Highness. So did the slapstick Santas tonight. You're the only person I know that calls me that, Barry. It's like your own little special nickname for me."

"It's not a nickname," he snarled. "Nicknames imply affection. I have absolutely no affection for anyone in your family. I detest every one of you."

"Yes, yes, I've heard it before. Don't you ever get sick of it? Don't you ever just feel like moving on with your life? Everyone else has."

"Never!" he swore. "Juliet Randolph made my grandmother an outcast. A child born out of wedlock, because Darwin Blakeslee married Juliet instead of Naomi! It put a blight against my family name. Back then, such a thing was scandalous."

"Okay, we'll go through this again, and maybe this time, some of it will sink in through that thick skull of yours. A) It happened over a hundred years ago. No one cares anymore. B) My family had nothing to do with it. We aren't even blood related to Juliet, so this family feud of yours is ridiculous. C) Above all, *I* had nothing to do with it. I wasn't even born yet. And D) You have wasted so much time and energy carrying this gigantic chip around on your shoulder for your entire life. Without it, you could have had a normal and happy life."

"Really? You think so?" he sneered. "You were always popular in high school. You were one of the golden ones. A Cessna. Everyone liked you. Things were different for me. I had to buy my friends," he spat bitterly. "I still do!"

"That's because you're a jerk, Barry, not because your grandmother was born out of wedlock!" Madison threw back at him.

"It doesn't matter what you say. Tonight, you and your boyfriend are going to die." His cold voice advanced in the darkness, alerting his captives he was moving closer. He continued with his mad rant. "He's another one of the golden ones. I don't know what my ancestor Bertram Randolph was thinking, *giving* a third of his plantation to a Mexican immigrant that worked for him!"

"FYI, the deCordovas are from Spain. And you really didn't listen during Texas history, did you, Barry? It so happens the Mexicans and Spaniards were here first. Andrew deCordova wasn't an immigrant; he was a hardworking and valuable employee who earned your great-great-grandfather's respect and gratitude. He knew Andrew would take care of the land and keep it prospering. He certainly couldn't depend on his squabbling daughters to do so."

From the darkness, Barry shone a bright light directly at her. At such close range, she could feel the heat of the beam upon her skin. Some of the brightness filtered through the blindfold she wore. "There you go, bad mouthing my family again!" he hissed. He reached out and ripped the material from her eyes, snatching out a handful of hair with the knotted fabric. Madison yelped in pain. She turned away from the light, certain she was not only blind, but also now bald.

"Look at me when I'm talking to you!" he screamed. "I'm going to teach you some humility before you die. When I'm done with you, you won't be a princess anymore."

She lifted her face toward him, but stubbornly kept her eyes shut.

"I never claimed to be a princess, Barry. But at least I'm not a toad, like you. That was the real clincher to revealing your identity, you know. I asked myself who was mean enough, and rotten enough, to steal Christmas presents from beneath people's trees? Who was greedy enough, and unconscionable enough, to head up an entire drug and gambling ring, no matter the damage it inflicted on other people? You've destroyed people's lives, Barry, with your greed and your sick, twisted mind."

"I'm the richest and most powerful man in The Sisters," he boasted. "In the entire county. It's been worth every sorry soul I had to sacrifice to get here. Even my own."

"You don't have a soul, Barry."

Her cavalier response enraged him. He slapped her so hard, her face jerked to one side. The noise resounded in the silence of the room.

The ratchet of a gun, loading a bullet into its barrel, was even louder.

"Touch her again," Brash ground out, his voice as hard as granite, "and I'll put a bullet through that sick brain of yours."

Barry jerked his light to the empty chair behind Madison. "Where—"

He got no further. With a deft move of his hands, Brash knew just the right pressure points to engage.

Barry Redmond crumpled to the floor in the sorry, undignified heap that he was.

"Brash!" Madison cried, jumping from the chair. Her hands were still bound and her phone slid to the floor, but the ropes fell from around her when she stood. "Oh my gosh, Brash, I was so scared!"

He held her to him in a tight squeeze. "You didn't act it. You were brilliant, Maddy. Brilliant! You probably saved our lives. Find your phone and call 9-1-1. Give me mine and I'll call, too, just as soon as I tie up this sorry piece of trash."

"I don't even know where my phone is," she fretted, too confused to think straight. "I can't see in the dark. Oh, there's my phone. Wait. Why is a light flashing?"

Cutter's voice floated through the darkness, from the vicinity of the doorway. "Because you've been live-streaming your conversation with Barry on the internet," he told her in amusement. "We couldn't see anything, but man, did we get an earful! Y'all okay in here? Where are the lights in this pile of junk?"

"Not connected. We need flashlights," Brash said, not bothering to look over his shoulder as he wound the smelly rope around Barry's prone body.

The fireman pulled a flashlight from his back pocket and pointed all nine hundred lumens at the ceiling, effectively lighting the entire room. "I didn't know what the situation was, so I walked in. The truck's back on the road."

"Good thinking. Call dispatch, tell them I need to set up a raid on Shubert Pharmacy. Better yet, call Vina at home. She'll know what to do. Tell her I need a search warrant and a SWAT team." Finished with Redmond, Brash finally looked up at his friend, who was already dialing his phone. "You want in?" he asked.

"You bet I do!" Cutter grinned. The phone connected and he turned serious. "Sorry to wake you, Miss Vina, but we have an emergency."

Across the room, Madison found her phone and turned off the live transmission button. "What did I do?" she wailed in despair. "I tried to call 9-1-1, but I couldn't see what I was doing. How on Earth did I manage to transmit over the internet?"

"I don't know, but I'm glad you did, sweetheart," Brash laughed. "You just broadcast his confession to the entire world. There's no way Barry Redmond can buy himself out of this one."

"I guess he didn't see the light on the phone. I was trying to keep it hidden." She rambled for a moment before she said worriedly, "What about the others, Brash? We have to stop them, too."

"Toss me my phone. I'll take it from here. And Maddy?"

"Yeah?"

"I love you, woman."

Despite the seriousness of the situation, Maddy ran to him and threw her still-bound hands around his neck, pulling his head down to hers. "I love you too." After a long and thorough kiss, she whispered, "Now, please cut me loose."

By the time daylight broke, the people of Naomi and Juliet were in shock.

Two of their most prestigious citizens were in custody, denied bail by a very cantankerous judge who had been awakened at two thirty in the morning to issue a search warrant. The pair was thrown behind bars alongside Bernie and Doug Havlicek, Dickey Fowler, Jaclyn Gonzales, and a half-dozen other accomplices rounded up in the raid. Tom Haskell was on the run, but it was only a matter of time before they hauled the career criminal back to Huntsville. Dickey had no problem rolling on him, telling the investigators anything they wanted to know, in hopes of cutting a deal.

Being among such common riffraff, as Granny Bert called them, was too much for Barry's ego to bear. When he tried but failed to hang himself with the bedsheets, it earned him a padded cell away from the others.

With Christmas now just three days away, Madison had no time to dwell on events from the night before. She had wrapping to do!

None of the gifts in Brash's truck had been fatally damaged or came up missing, so she had that to be thankful for. She locked herself and all her gifts inside her suite of rooms and went on a wrapping frenzy. By the time Brash stopped by, worn and weary after thirty-eight hours on his feet, she was officially done. With his help, she transferred the presents downstairs and placed them beneath the family tree in the media room.

"This is going to be an awesome Christmas," she whispered, accepting his kiss beside the twinkling lights. "Our first Christmas together."

"The first of many to come, I hope," he murmured.

"Yes, please."

"We're still on for Christmas morning, right?"

"Yes. We have Christmas Eve at noon with your family, dinner at Granny Bert's, Christmas morning here, noon at Shannon's, then dinner again here with our friends."

"I don't know whether to starve myself for the next two days, or eat as much as I can and stretch my stomach. That's a lot of Christmas dinners and desserts in just two days," Brash laughed.

"I know. Isn't it great?" She hugged him, her heart filled with joy. "Last Christmas was such a blur. The last two or three Christmas have been, if I'm being honest. I can't remember the last time I was looking forward to the holiday this much."

"I hope you won't be disappointed."

"You'll be here, won't you?"

"Definitely."

"Then I won't be disappointed. In fact, I don't care if I don't get a single gift. As long as you, Bethani, Blake, and Megan are all here, I have everything I need. Having my parents here is like the bow on top of my perfect present."

"Hey, why didn't you tell me this before I bought your gift?" he teased. "I could have saved thirty-five bucks!"

"Very funny, mister. And totally fine. Love is supposed to be free, after all."

"And best of all, mine comes with a money-back guarantee. At the end of ninety-nine years, if you aren't completely satisfied, you get your full investment back."

"Ninety-nine years, huh? Sounds like a solid deal. Can I get that in writing?"

Brash fought the urge to go down on one knee, right then and there. But he didn't have the ring back. Yet. He talked to the judge and the DA, and both had agreed to release the ring before Christmas, so that he could give it to her as planned. He knew Megan was looking forward to being part of their special moment. It was important to him to include their children in their marriage, right from the start.

Reining in his enthusiasm, he dropped a kiss onto her nose and promised, "In triplicate."

Christmas morning would be here soon enough.

21

Snow on Christmas was never an option in east central Texas, but at least December 25 dawned cold and frosty. So often, it was warm on the holiday, but this year was a pleasant exception.

Madison was up early, bustling about in the kitchen while she prepped for breakfast. Keeping with a tradition she and Gray had started when the twins were toddlers, she crept up the stairs and hung a stocking on each of their doors.

When the children were little, the stockings were filled with token toys and small pieces of candy or fruit, meant to appease them in their rooms as their parents put the final changes on gifts from Santa. As the twins matured, so did the presents, morphing into stickers and colored pens and puzzles and such. They still received stockings on the mantel, but these were their pre-stockings, as Blake liked to call them.

This year had been particularly challenging. At sixteen, their tastes had evolved beyond Madison's meager budget. Still, there were nail polishes and hair ribbons for Bethani, fishing gadgets and a small flashlight for Blake. The rest of their gifts were tucked into their official stockings, or wrapped in pretty paper beneath the tree.

Brash and Megan arrived promptly at eight o'clock, their arms filled with boxes. Cutter arrived soon behind him, his arms just as full.

"You're sure you don't mind me and Genny tagging along onto your Christmas?" Cutter asked, tucking his fiancé under his arm once he deposited the gifts.

Madison put her hands onto her hips. "If you ask me that question one more time, I'm going to lie and tell you yes, I do mind. Now not another word. Like it or not, you and Genny are family."

"Okay," he grinned, "but I can't promise we'll be here next year on Christmas morning." He smiled down at the love of his life. "I'd like to think we might be celebrating our own baby's first Christmas by then."

"Don't get ahead of yourself, big guy!" Genny laughed, blushing prettily. "Let's get through the wedding, before we start planning a family."

"February fourteenth can't come too soon for me. I wish it was yesterday, so we'd already be married by now."

"Aw, what a sweet thing to say," Madison smiled. "I still say you're cheating yourself out of a present every year, Genny, being that your anniversary will be Valentine's Day, but whatever makes you happy makes me happy."

Genny beamed up at her handsome and younger boyfriend. "This guy right here," she admitted. "He's what makes me happy."

Feeling the same about Brash, Madison nodded in full understanding. "I love the new pajamas he gave you, by the way."

Genny's newest sleepshirt was fire-engine red and said, 'I'm so hot, I come with my own firefighter' emblazoned across the front.

Keeping to tradition, all the women were still in their nightclothes for gifts and breakfast. Madison wore a demure and modest peignoir set in filmy moss green, a perfect complement for her coloring. Blake, Bethani, and Megan all wore matching Christmas pajamas. They were Christmas Eve gifts from their respective parents, who had selected the outfits together. Happy wore a flowing set of simple white robes, but topped it off with a festive Santa hat. Granny, who hadn't planned to come until Brash made a secret and special request for her presence, came in her flannel gown and robe.

They opened stockings first, and then had breakfast. As they devoured breakfast casseroles and baked French toast, crispy strips of bacon and fat sausages, scrambled eggs, and southern-style grits, the doorbell rang. Not expecting anyone else until this evening, Madison asked Brash to see who it was while she put on another pot of coffee.

He swung the door open with a hearty greeting of, "Merry Christmas!"

A well-dressed couple stood on the threshold, their faces set in surprise. The woman was decked out in all her Christmas finery, a shiny ensemble of muted golds and red. She was wrapped in a full mink coat and had diamonds on all her fingers and pearls at her neck. The man beside her wore a dark blue business suit, snazzed up for the holiday with a festive red handkerchief and matching tie, both hand-embroidered with tiny mistletoe.

"May I help you?" Brash asked, thinking the well-to-do couple must be lost.

"Are you the butler?" the woman asked frostily, her eyes sweeping over his casual attire with obvious disdain. Maddy had fully approved of his snug-fitting jeans and solid red western shirt, but not this woman. She peered at him down her aristocratic nose, which was quite an impressive feat, considering he towered over her.

"Hardly!" he laughed. "Actually, I'm the chief of police. Is there something I can help with you?"

"Yes. You can tell our grandchildren we're here to see them. And you can fetch the gifts from the car, if you please."

Brash's heart sank. This was hardly the audience he had intended for his grand proposal.

"Well? Are you just going to stand there, or are you going to allow us inside?" the woman demanded. "This is our daughter-in-law's home, is it not? Madison Reynolds."

"Yes, this is Maddy's home," he said smoothly. He held out his hand to the other man. "You must be Blake and Bethani's grandparents. Brash deCordova."

"Charles Reynolds. This is my wife, Annette."

There were no false pleasantries, no empty 'nice to meet you' from either side. Sizing each other up like opponents on a wrestling mat, Brash kept his gaze steady and pensive as he studied first Charles, and then Annette. He didn't want to overstep his bounds, but he was certain by this time next year, this would be his home, too. Sooner than that, if he had a say in the matter. And he was equally certain he knew how Madison would feel about her in-laws being here today. She would tolerate them for her children's sake, just as Brash was willing to do. But there was no way in Santa's wonderland he would allow them to walk all over or to verbally abuse the woman he loved. The sooner he made that clear to them, the better.

"We're having breakfast before we open presents. Would you care to join us?"

"I hardly think it's your place to invite us for breakfast," Annette sniffed. "You don't live here. Or do you?" She added the last with pointed accusation.

"No, but I'm a frequent guest. I believe this is your first time to visit, correct?" He followed the smooth reprimand with one of his more charming smiles. "It's a gorgeous old home, don't you think?"

He kept them standing in the cold until they agreed with him.

"You can put your coat away through there," he suggested, motioning toward a small closet beneath the stairs. He didn't want her mistaking him for the butler again.

Annette looked at him in confusion. She was unaccustomed to people who dared not jump at her every command. She turned to her husband for support—or perhaps to have him hang her coat for her—but he kept his eyes trained on Brash. When Brash saw a nerve twitch in the older man's cheek, he realized Charles was trying hard not to smile at the handling of his wife.

Maybe the old guy wasn't so bad, after all, Brash decided. Just hen-pecked by an overbearing woman.

"Go ahead, Annette, it will be fine," Charles said, eyes straight ahead.

She stalked forward with a huff. With her back to him, Charles' smile broke through. Brash offered a conspiratorial wink, surprised when the older man nodded his approval.

"I hope you're hungry," Brash said, offering his arm to Annette once her mink and her purse were safely tucked away. "Maddy and Genny have been cooking all morning. There's plenty, so come on into the kitchen and join us."

"The kitchen?" Annette sounded appalled. In their household, only the servants ate in the kitchen.

"Don't worry, we'll have dinner tonight in the formal dining room, but the kitchen is so much cozier. Perfect for family meals, don't you think?" He kept up the firm but friendly discourse, subtly putting Annette into her place. She was on Maddy's turf now, and she would treat it, and her, with respect. Charles tagged behind, openly smiling.

Brash pushed through the swinging kitchen doors, hoping for the best. "Set two more plates for breakfast, Maddy. You have more guests."

Conversation around the table stopped. A fork clattered onto a plate. Madison stared at her former in-laws with dismay. Her first thought was to wonder who had invited them. Her second thought was as to why Annette's hand was tucked into the crook of Brash's arm. Charles stood behind them, grinning like a Cheshire cat full of cream.

"Grandmother Annette! Grandfather!" Bethani broke the silence with her delighted cry. She jumped up from the table and came forward, but Brash noticed she stopped short of hugging them. "I didn't think you'd really come! Merry Christmas!"

He quickly stepped aside. "Here, Beth, I'll get out of your way so you can hug your grandparents."

Brash smiled serenely at Annette as he slipped past her. He made a quick path to Maddy, where he stood close behind her and whispered, "I didn't know whether to slam the door in their faces or let them in, but it is Christmas. Good will to men and warty old mother-in-laws, and all that." He referred to a conversation they had once had about her, when Madison had compared Annette to a witch. After meeting her in person, he saw the resemblance.

"There goes my perfect Christmas," she whispered back.

"Not a chance. We won't let them spoil this. Agreed?"

With a quick prayer for strength, Maddy gave a tight nod. "Agreed."

They made room for the newcomers and passed food their way. Annette turned her nose up at most of the offerings, but one taste of Genny's baked French toast and she fell under its spell. She melted like the butter atop the warm, gooey mess.

"I simply must have this recipe to give to Cook," she said, all but licking her plate clean.

"I'd be happy to show you how to make it, Annette," Genny offered.

"Annette doesn't cook," Charles corrected immediately. "We have help for that."

"Ooh, I see a cooking class in this afternoon's future!" Genny grinned, rubbing her hands together. She had noticed how Brash handled the overbearing woman, and it seemed to work. Treat her like an ordinary human being rather than a queen to be patronized, and she almost behaved as one. "Bethani and Megan can help. This will be fun!"

After breakfast, everyone pitched in to make quick work of the dishes. To her amazement, Madison saw Annette actually carry her own coffee cup and plate to the sink. Wonders, she thought with a daze, would never cease.

With the kitchen clean and the dishwashers running, they returned to the media room. Brash went out to collect the gifts from the Reynolds' classic Rolls Royce, the one Blake said they only drove on special occasions. He counted exactly four presents, two apiece for each of the twins. Nothing for Maddy.

Once everyone assembled in the media room, the men passed out presents. As the piles of presents grew, so did the noise level in the room. Christmas music played on the sound system, often drowned out by laughter and squeals of delight. Brash took a seat by Madison, where the two preferred to watch the pleasure on everyone else's faces, rather than open their own presents.

"Go ahead, Brash," she smiled, nudging his shoulder. "Open your gifts."

"I already did, the day I re-met you inside Ronny Gleason's chicken house," he said softly.

"I beg your pardon, but we were outside the house, where I was puking my guts up after finding him dead."

"So we were."

"Seriously, open something, or we'll be here all day."

"You, too."

They selected one present each, and tore away the colorful paper.

Few others in the room used such restraint.

"Mom, thank you, thank you, thank you! Just what I wanted!" Blake cried in excitement when he opened his rod and reel. "Mr. de, Cutter, can we go fishing this afternoon?"

"Not this afternoon, buddy," Brash laughed. "But maybe tomorrow."

"What a cute sweater, Miss Maddy! I love it!" Megan beamed, coming forward to hug the giver.

"I thought it would go great with your coloring." Maddy touched the girl's long, auburn locks, her hand lingering with affection.

Across the room, she saw Annette watching her. Instead of the normal criticism, her mother-in-law's eyes held a thoughtful gaze. The normally vocal woman had said little since joining them in their noisy, happy ritual of opening gifts en mass. At Ivy Hall, the pompous name Annette had given their cold and stately home, Christmas get-togethers had never been like this, not even when the twins were younger. There, they gathered around the professionally decorated tree and opened presents one by one, politely waiting on the person to their left to finish unwrapping a gift before starting on their own. Discarded paper was neatly folded and tucked away, not torn and wadded and thrown to the middle of the room for later disposal. Some were even wrapped like they were on television, with lift-off lids, complete with stationary bows and ribbons. And there were never more than two gifts apiece. Three, at absolute tops, and only if your name wasn't Madison. One year, there hadn't been a single gift with her name upon it, a fact that Annette swore was the maid's fault. Her promise to bring the present by later never quite materialized. Just one of the many snubs Madison had endured during her twenty-year marriage to their son.

"Mom, seriously?" Bethani squealed. "It's just what I wanted!" She pulled the expensive hair straightener from the box, brandishing the sparkly pink wand for everyone to see. "I can't wait to use this!"

Round and round it went, as everyone opened their gifts at once. When the twins opened their first gifts from their

Dallas grandparents, they had to do so in tandem. They each lifted out a big, puffy snowsuit, one in pink, one in blue.

"Thanks," Blake said, wondering why he needed such a suit in Texas. "It looks really warm and poufy."

"It should be just the right weight for Colorado," Charles said, seeing his confusion. "We'd like to take you to Vail for snow skiing."

"Are you kidding me? That's awesome!" the teen replied with new enthusiasm. He shook the suit out for closer inspection.

"Bethani? Do you like your suit?" Annette answered, noticing her lack-luster response to the invitation.

The teen darted a glance at her best friend. She knew how badly Megan wanted to go snow skiing. It was something she had never done before, but had it at the top of her bucket list. Bethani felt guilty about going without her friend, especially when she herself really didn't care for the sport all that much.

"Oh, sure. I love the color. Good call." She darted another look at Megan, who was trying hard to hide her jealousy.

The unbelievable happened when Annette took one look at Megan's crestfallen face, glanced at her granddaughter's look of guilt and sadness, and made a momentous offer. "Bethani, would you like to invite your friend to come along? I'm sure I can find her a suit like yours in purple."

Bethani's blue eyes sparkled. "Really, Grandmother Annette? Are you serious?"

"Why yes, if her father agrees."

"Can I, Daddy? Please, oh please?" Megan got on her knees and made begging noises, which Bethani soon echoed.

"I suppose so, if your mother says yes."

"Yes!" The girls jumped up and hugged first Brash for agreeing, then Annette and Charles for the gift. Annette accepted the hugs, looking slightly dazed by so much show of affection. When they finally settled back into their places on the floor, she patted her perfectly styled hair back into place, but a faint smile lingered on her lips.

The second gift from their grandparents brought even more hugs, even from Blake. The latest iPhone winked up at them from the tissue.

Seeing the instant worry on Madison's face, Charles was quick to assure her. "The bill will come to us, of course. And we'll buy out any contract you have on their old phones."

His words were a relief. It was a struggle to pay their current phone bill, the one she had trimmed to the bare necessities. "That's very generous of you. Thank you."

In truth, it was the first thing they had ever done to ease the financial burden left to her by their son. Sure, they had paid off his debt to the IRS, but that was to save his good name, not to help her in any fashion. But it was Christmas, Madison reminded herself. No time to be petty. She would be thankful for any help they threw her way.

At last, there was just one gift left unopened, a huge box wrapped in colorful angel paper and bearing Madison's name.

"I can't wait to see what this is," she said. She had already opened three other presents from Brash and Megan. "As big as it is, please tell me there's not a live animal inside." She darted a look at her daughter and asked in mock horror, "It's not that pony you promised Bethani, is it?"

The girls giggled at the reference, but Brash looked suddenly uncertain. He avoided looking at Annette and Charles.

Because of their unexpected presence today, he stalled. "Uhm, maybe you should wait until later to open that one."

"Are you kidding? No way! I've been dying of curiosity, ever since you brought this bad boy in!"

"Well... okay," he agreed reluctantly. He pulled it easily within her reach.

"Is it heavy?" she asked, lifting the corner to test its weight. "Hmm, not so much. Does it rattle?" She jiggled it, but nothing sounded from within.

"Open it, already!" someone called with a laugh.

"Okay, here goes." Madison pulled away the paper and pried the tape away, opening the big box. A slightly smaller box rested inside, wrapped in blue snowflakes.

"Okay, here goes, again." She repeated the process, only to find a box bearing golden stars. She shot Brash an evil look, but he only laughed at her frustration.

"And again," she said, finding still another box, this one swathed in a snowy Christmas scene upon a green background.

"Trick wrapping!" Cutter called.

Maddy's eyes flew to meet Brash's, recalling how Marilyn Bashinski had wrapped the watch for her husband. Brash waggled his brows playfully, but she saw the light in his dark eyes. Her heart kicked into overdrive.

The fifth box was quite a bit smaller, and wrapped in metallic red. The room drew oddly quiet as she tore away the wrappings, her hands just a bit unsteady. *It could be a watch*, she reminded herself.

But nestled inside the white tissue was a tiny velvet box, too small to hold a watch. *Earrings*, she cautioned her racing heart, but she raised hopeful eyes to Brash's bright, inquisitive gaze.

Taking an unsteady breath, she reached inside and lifted out the box, drawing soft gasps from those who watched. When her hands became too unreliable to manage the lid, Brash took it from her and went down on one knee. Maddy cried out softly, tears already pricking her eyes. Her head was already doing a tiny warble. No one, not even her, was sure if it was from nerves or eagerness.

"Madison Josephine Cessna Reynolds, I love you with all my heart and soul," Brash said in a voice strong and rich, yet at the same time soft and gentle. "I can't imagine living my life without you by my side. I've talked to our children. We all agree that we're a perfect fit. So, Megan and I have something to ask you. Will you, Madison Reynolds, marry us? Will you, and Blake and Bethani, become a part of our family, and let us be part of yours?" A devilish light slipped into his adoring gaze. "And before you answer me, remember that money-back guarantee that comes with my love. In triplicate."

No one else understood his reference, other than Madison. But she needed no guarantee in triplicate. She saw it within his eyes.

"Yes! Yes, yes, yes, of course I'll marry you!" she cried, grabbing his handsome face in both her hands. She peppered him all over with kisses. "*We'll* marry you! Won't we, Blake and Bethani?" She didn't wait for their answer, just motioned them forward as she kissed him full on the mouth to seal the deal.

Amid laughter and hugs and congratulations all around, Madison and Brash gathered with their three children and made promises for a future together. Almost as an afterthought, Brash slipped the ring onto her finger. It was a perfect fit, just as he knew it would be.

"There's actually a funny story behind this ring," he told her, "but I'll save that for later. Right this moment, I'd like to kiss my fiancé, if you don't mind."

"Actually," she murmured, "I'd mind if you didn't."

22

L ate in the afternoon, Madison stepped into a busy kitchen, alive with delicious aromas, buoyant chatter, and hearty laughter. Blake was at the center of it all, telling some animated tale that had the entire room entertained.

"Ah, and here she is now, back from her famous ring tour!" he announced dramatically, catching sight of his mother in the doorway.

The teen had given the silly name to their frenzy of mid-day activity. Some of the stops had been pre-arranged—Shannon and Matt's, for one—but some had been spontaneous, in part to announce their good news to people like Brash's parents and his sister. After rounds of best wishes for the holidays and blessings for their future, they were finally back at the Big House, where preparations were well underway for the last of the day's activities. Dinner here was scheduled for seven thirty.

"Very cute," she told her son. She eyed a half-eaten slice of pie on the plate he held. "And please don't tell me you are seriously eating again, when we've spent the day gorging our-selves and have another meal in two hours!"

"Had to replenish my energy sources after that crazy tour around the countryside. If this is what it feels like to be a mov-ie star, I may reconsider my career choices." He popped the rest of the pie into his mouth in one large bite.

"Movie star? I thought you were teetering between playing professional baseball and tournament fishing."

"Hey, a guy's gotta keep his options open. My drama teach-er says I have a gift. She says I'm full of potential."

"You're full of something, all right," his sister retorted. She and Megan were busy chopping vegetables at Genny's direc-tive, right alongside Happy and, to Madison's utter surprise, Annette.

Not only had she not seen Annette set foot in a kitchen in years, but their mothers had never gotten along well, hers and Gray's. Yet here both women were, offering their limited skills of cooking while actually being civil to one another. A Christmas Day miracle, Madison mused.

"Sorry it took me so long to get in here," Madison apolo-gized, primarily to Genny. In deference to her expertise, ev-eryone looked to the blonde as the main chef, a fact Madison felt guilty about. This was her kitchen, after all. "And you didn't have to do all this yet. You could have waited on me to do my part."

"Honestly, it wasn't a big deal," her best friend assured her. "I wanted to do a little prepping now, so that later all we have to do is put it all together. Cutter and I are going to slip out to the house for a minute so he can show me something." He was remodeling his grandparent's old farmhouse, where they would live after the wedding.

Right on cue, the fireman popped into the room. He made a shh-ing motion with his hand and slipped up behind her where she stood at the stove, stirring a pot of beans that would soon be mashed and turned into refried beans. Slipping his arms around her waist, he dropped a kiss onto the back of her neck.

"Hey, gorgeous, what's cooking?"

Jumping slightly in surprise, she took his playful banter in stride and dryly warned, "Your goose, if you sneak up on me like that again."

"Hey, Maddy, mind if I steal the love of my life away for a minute? I have one last Christmas surprise for her. I promise we won't be too long."

"Not at all. Genny, tell me what to do and we'll take it from here."

Genny glanced around at what was already done. "Why don't we let the kids finish prepping these vegetables, and you ladies set the table in the dining room? I don't know what dishes you want to use. After that, take a load off and enjoy a few minutes of downtime. We'll get down to some serious cooking when I get back." She untied her apron and revealed a frilly red dress, perfect for the holiday.

"No rush," Maddy told her. "We've got this."

"Don't let my beans scorch," Genny warned on her way out the door.

"Blake, keep an eye on the beans," his mother directed. "Stir them every so often. I'll get the plates."

She stepped into the butler's pantry and studied her choices. As a promotional tool, sponsors had filled the glass-fronted cabinets with dishes in an array of colors and patterns, most of which she would never use. After careful thought, she selected six place settings of solid red, and six from her own china pattern of white-on-white.

The china was from her wedding registry. Madison had always thought it a silly tradition, asking friends to spend a ridiculous amount of money to buy fancy dishes used only on rare occasions. She had never been a china and stemware kind of girl—her own mother relied on paper plates and Tupperware tumblers, while Granny Bert used a mishmash of stoneware and melamine—but Annette insisted it was tradition to choose a china pattern, so choose a pattern she did. Her soon-to-be mother-in-law encouraged her to select something neutral, to better stand the test of time. It was one of the few pieces of good advice Annette had ever offered.

Madison gathered the dishes, along with her good silverware, another frivolous item from her gift registry. The remainder of the dishes would come from the china cabinet in the formal dining room.

It was difficult to decorate a room dominated by the masterpiece upon its wall. Even Kinky Paretta knew to keep it simple, relying on polished antique furnishings and burnished pewter to complement the artist's work.

For a touch of Christmas cheer in the impressive room, Madison used evergreen garlands strung from the chandeliers, red candles and coordinating ribbons in all the appropriate places, and her prized Christmas china. That, she always believed, had not been a frivolous purchase.

A bittersweet smile touched her face as she pulled the needed place settings from her collection. Gray had given her a starter set of the dishes on their first Christmas together, then added a few pieces every year after that for a handful of years. She remembered her delight when she opened that first box and found the pattern she had coveted for so long.

As a little girl, she thought of Christmas dishes as the ultimate symbol of stability. They moved often when she was a child, following Charlie's whims as he went from one career to the next. She loved her father dearly, but a stable family man he was not. In her mind, to live in the same house year after year and to celebrate the holidays with a set of Christmas dishes was the sign of a normal life. Young Madison craved normal.

Marriage to Grayson Reynolds promised a life of normalcy, or so she hoped. The dishes were proof. But somewhere along the way—perhaps around the time he stopped adding to her collection—their lives became more complicated. Their priorities shifted. Schedules turned chaotic. Greed and ambition reared their ugly heads. Simple things like Christmas dishes no longer seemed so important, not in the overall scheme of things. Even before Gwendolyn came into their lives, Madison had bought the final few pieces of the collection herself, determined to complete her set.

She didn't notice when her mother-in-law stepped into the room, until she heard her voice. "You always did like those dishes."

Madison touched a plate with reverence. "I think it was possibly the best gift Gray ever gave me," she said.

Annette's voice sounded somewhat strangled. "Did you ever really love my son?"

Madison's stricken gaze flew to hers. "How can you even ask that? Of course, I loved Gray! Don't you remember how happy we were when we first married? When the twins were born? I worshiped the ground he walked on, and vice versa!"

"Then what happened?" Annette demanded.

Instead of immediately answering, Madison walked slowly around the table, setting a Christmas plate down at every other spot. The places in between would be set with alternating solid red or white plates, topped with bowls or salad plates in the Christmas pattern. It was an informal, mismatched way of sharing her beloved dishes with each person present. No doubt, Annette would disapprove of her table setting. After all, it was an unconventional means of compromise, and completely untraditional. That was one of the reasons Madison loved the idea the moment it occurred to her.

About the second plate, Madison began her slow and painful reply. "Don't you think I've asked myself that question a thousand times? I don't know what happened, Annette, other than to say that life happened. We both became so busy. Gray with work, first at the bank, then with our own agency, trying to snag and keep clients. I was busy trying to be the perfect wife and mother, trying to do it all—running a household, being a taxi service for the twins, a secretary for Gray, a hostess for our social life. We let *things* come between us. Things that weren't nearly as important as one another. And we didn't even realize it, until it was too late. And by then..." Her voice trailed off in sadness.

"If you had tried harder—"

"No, Annette." Madison broke in before she could say more, her gentle voice allowing no argument. "I did try. It just wasn't working anymore. Our marriage was broken." She picked up a stack of red plates and retraced her steps around the extended table. She drew a resolute breath into her lungs. "But that is in the past, and it can never be undone. I'm moving forward now, with Brash."

"It's just so soon. It's only been a year," Gray's mother sobbed softly, dabbing at her eyes.

"I know today has been awkward for you. And I know it must hurt, seeing a new man in our lives. I'm sorry for that, I truly am, but I hope you can find it in your heart to be happy for us."

To her surprise, Annette turned a hand in setting the table. She followed behind her with a stack of white plates, filling in the missing spaces.

Annette's extraordinary effort to bend demanded that she reciprocate. "It was nice of you and Charles to come," Madison said. "I know it meant a lot to Blake and Bethani, having their grandparents here for Christmas."

"Bethani invited us, you know." A bit of defensiveness slipped back into her voice.

"Yes, I know. And it's fine. Really." Madison made a third pass around the table, alternating salad plates and bowls. The menu didn't include soup, but the bowls could hold chips and salsa. "What you did for Megan today was very kind and generous. Thank you for that."

"She appears to be a good girl. Polite and respectful."

"She was raised by a good man."

Unwilling to bend too far, Annette only allowed, "For the children's sake, I certainly hope so."

"You and Charles are welcome to spend the night. Blake and Bethani would love to have you."

"We might consider it."

"Please do. Genny might even let you help make her baked French toast again for breakfast." She added the last bit, knowing it would be hard to resist. Oddly enough, she truly wanted them to stay over and spend time with their grandchildren.

Annette gave a slight nod as she picked up the silverware and the napkins. "I'll speak with Charles."

They gathered round the table for their Christmas evening meal, a new tradition among this hodgepodge of kinfolk, blended families, and dear friends.

Brash insisted that Madison take the head of the table. Next year, he told her with a sexy wink, he might not be so generous. Seating himself beside her, he suggested that Blake take the other end. The show of respect earned Brash high points with the flattered teenager, his starry-eyed mother, and even a begrudging Annette.

Stretched between mother and son were all the people that mattered most in their lives. Bethani and Brash, of course, and Megan, Genny, and Granny Bert. Cutter was there with his grandfather Sticker, and Shannon and Matt with their young son. Madison purposely seated Derron beside Annette, knowing her friendly and entertaining employee never met a stranger. If anyone could charm the woman into the Christmas spirit, it was Derron. Charles sat next to Charlie, and Happy sat between him and Sherika Green. Jamil, his parents, and his three siblings couldn't be excluded from the new tradition, any more than Andy and Lydia deCordova could.

It was a noisy, cheerful meal, served with laughter and spiced with love.

Before they had dessert—a sinful array of candies, pies, cakes, and puddings, and topped off by Genny's special chocolate-drizzled tres leches cake—Madison stood to make a toast. She asked her children to stand with her.

"I want to thank each one of you for being here and sharing this night with us, and for helping our family as we begin a new tradition, one for our new life here in The Sisters. This year has been... difficult for us, to say the least," her eyes trailed briefly to her former in-laws, "filled with heartache and challenges. At times, it has tested our strength and our faith and yes, our very sanity." As her admission drew a laugh from the table, she sucked in a shaky breath and forged onward.

"But it has also been filled with so many wonderful and unexpected rewards. The most precious of those rewards sit with us here tonight. Moving back here to Juliet to live with my dear grandmother has proved to be the wisest decision I have ever made as a mother. I have watched my children grow and flourish amid this closely knit community. They've made new friends, discovered new talents, stretched their wings, and become the amazing young adults their father and I always knew they could be. If you'll just allow me this one weepy moment... Blake, Bethani, your father would be so proud of you if he could see you now. Don't ever forget how much he loved and adored both of you."

Amid sniffs scattered throughout the room, Madison wiped away her own tears and smiled. "But enough of the sadness. Tonight is about new traditions, new happiness, and new friends. Not, of course, that we're doing away with the old. I couldn't have survived this past year without my best and dearest friend Genny. She's been my rock."

When Madison lifted her glass to Genny and everyone cheered, Cutter slipped his arm around his fiancé's shoulders and beamed, "She is amazing, isn't she?"

"Granny, you've been my foundation, ever since I was a little girl. Thank you for giving that same firm and loving foundation to my children. Mom, Dad, thank you for having the wisdom to allow me to spend my teenage years here with Granny Bert." She lifted her glass to each of them in turn.

Her attention settled upon Brash, and emotion overcame her again. "And this man right here... What can I say? There are no words. But in case you missed the gorgeous ring on my finger or this big, crazy smile on my face, I am beyond thrilled to say that Blake, Bethani, and I are marrying Brash and his beautiful daughter Megan."

Brash stood and slipped his arm around her waist, sweeping her into a quick, hard kiss. He stayed beside her as the applause died and she concluded her speech.

"I can honestly say that I have never been happier in my entire life, and I owe it all to the people in this room. Thank you, dear friends and family, for all that you have given to us." She hugged Brash's side and swept her gaze around the room, lingering on the faces of her precious children.

"I can hardly wait to see what the coming year has in store for us! Merry Christmas, dear friends, and the happiest of New Year's!"

Echoing Maddy, I wish each of you a wonderful and happy holiday season. Please stay tuned for new adventures coming to The Sisters in 2018!

NOTE FROM THE AUTHOR

As always, thank you for reading! I hope this story has given you an enjoyable escape. If you would like to return the favor, please consider the gift of a review. No matter the season, it is the best present possible for any author.

Contrary to recent rumors circulating in reviews, the series is not ending, not as long as you wonderful readers continue to support it.

Feel free to contact me at beckiwillis.ccp@gmail.com, or through the links below.

https://www.beckiwillis.com
https://www.facebook.com/beckiwillis.ccp/
https://www.facebook.com/theSisters.texas/
https://twitter.com/beckiwillis15

ABOUT THE AUTHOR

Becki Willis, best known for her popular The Sisters, Texas Mystery Series and Forgotten Boxes, always dreamed of being an author. In November of '13, that dream became a reality. Since that time, she has published numerous books, won first place honors for Best Mystery Series, Best Suspense Fiction and Best Audio Book, and has introduced her imaginary friends to readers around the world.

An avid history buff, Becki likes to poke around in old places and learn about the past. Other addictions include reading, writing, junking, unraveling a good mystery, and coffee. She loves to travel, but believes coming home to her family and her Texas ranch is the best part of any trip. Becki is a member of the Association of Texas Authors, the National Association of Professional Women, and the Brazos Writers organization. She attended Texas A&M University and majored in Journalism.

You can connect with her at http://www.beckiwillis.com/ and http://www.facebook.com/beckiwillis.ccp?ref=hl. Better yet, email her at beckiwillis.ccp@gmail.com. She loves to hear from readers and encourages feedback!

Here's what readers are saying about Becki and her books: "This is an awesome new author with a strong voice! This was a great read with tons of suspense and great character development. I highly recommend you read this author!"... "The best new series available."... "Full of twists and the best love story revealed in ages. Loved it!"..."I should know better than to start one of Becki's books at bedtime. So hard to stop in the middle!"..."I loved every line of every page!!!"

Made in the USA
San Bernardino, CA
15 August 2020

77078289R00140

Made in the USA
San Bernardino, CA
15 August 2020